THE STORY OF  Tönle

Tönle

THE STORY OF

MARIO RIGONI STERN

TRANSLATED FROM THE ITALIAN
BY JOHN SHEPLEY

T M P

THE MARLBORO PRESS/NORTHWESTERN
NORTHWESTERN UNIVERSITY PRESS
EVANSTON, ILLINOIS

The Marlboro Press/Northwestern
Northwestern University Press
www.nupress.northwestern.edu

Printed in the United States of America

ISBN 978-0-8101-6093-4

The Library of Congress has cataloged the original, hardcover edition as follows:

Rigoni Stern, Mario.
    [Storia di Tönle. English]
    The story of Tönle / Mario Rigoni Stern ; translated from the Italian by John Shepley.
       p. cm.
    ISBN 978-0-8101-6034-x (cloth : alk. paper)
    I. Shepley, John. II. Title.
    PQ4878.I3S713 1998
    853'914—dc21   98-9910
                                          CIP

Every evening there was a cow, gazing motionless, on the slopes of the Moor. She stood out against the clear sky above the horizon, her pedestal being the mound of earth dug from the mountain in the spring of 1916 to make way for a battery of heavy artillery.

Sad and intent, huddled in his wicker armchair and wrapped in a blanket to protect himself from the cold air, Gigi Ghirotti also gazed in silence.

"What's that cow looking at?" he muttered. "And what does she think about? I see her there every night. Maybe," he added, as I kept silent, "she wants to get her fill of sights and sounds at this time, for when snow and cold will keep her shut up for months in the stable. Or for when she's dead."

"Maybe," I replied, "she's waiting to see the sun come up. Can't you see she always looks east?"

Meanwhile, from the woods and mountain, night was descending on us; but even in the darkness, against the starry sky, the cow stood motionless and gazing. She was like time itself.

It was then that I began telling Gigi the story of Tönle Bintarn.

ONE

At the edge of the wood, wary as a wild animal waiting for dusk before emerging into the open, he gazed at his hamlet, and over the wide stretch of meadows the town below it. Fragrant wood smoke dissolved in the pink and violet sky where flocks of crows flew, cawing to one other.

On the roof of his house was a tree: a wild cherry tree. The seed from which it had grown had landed up there when a redwing expelled it in flight many years before, and springtime conditions had made it sprout because his grandfather, to protect the house from rain and snow, had spread extra thatch on the roof so that underneath it had become humus and almost sod. Thus the cherry tree had grown.

Tönle Bintarn, as he gazed, recalled how as a boy, after the rye harvest, he would climb up from the side of the stable where the wide roof almost met the slope of the mountain, and one by one pick all the sweet, black little cherries before the blackbirds and thrushes came with their beaks: they were like honey, and for days the juice stains stayed on his hands and around his mouth, and the water from the Prunnele stream wasn't enough to remove it. But in the fall the pale red of the leaves could be seen even from the top of the Moor, like an oriflamme that ennobled the humble house and distinguished it from the others.

Now, on this December evening, the branches stood out against the sky like a hieroglyph, and if it hadn't been for the light smoke issuing from the stone vents under the projections of the roofs, the houses of the hamlet would have been scarcely visible against the snow-covered ground. (Our houses, at that time, had no chimney pots: a flue led from the main room to the attic, where sparks were extinguished by a basket of sticks plastered with clay; the smoke, spreading throughout the attic, maintained a welcome heat above the house and also cured and hardened the larchwood beams of the trusses, preserving them over the centuries.)

He had been away for nine months, and had sent news of himself one day from Regensburg on meeting a fellow countryman who was on his way back to Italy. Here's what had happened.

As always, ever since he was no longer a child, he had had to make two or three trips a month every winter transporting various items across the border. From there he brought back hobnailed shoes for men and articles of clothing for women, from here he carried sugarloaves, spirits, and twists of tobacco. When things went well, he was able to earn enough in one trip to buy a bushel of barley or cornmeal, a pot of sharp cheese, or a couple of dried codfish.

But this trade didn't always go smoothly, for since 1866 the easy crossing points had been guarded by revenue agents of the Kingdom of Italy, who didn't always let you through, and at the cry "Halt!" you had to drop your load and run. But it also happened that organized groups of smugglers managed to pass through checkpoints that had been secretly agreed on beforehand, by dropping in a guard's cap the toll of one silver lira for each load of goods.

Tönle got together with four companions from the hamlet, and wherever possible they followed the tracks of the logging sleds, after which they entered the depths of the woods, and to avoid leaving footprints they walked under the trees where the snow is always harder; higher up they followed a line of cliffs as far as the border. The danger lay in going down the other side into the territory of Franz Josef, not because of the Austrian gendarmes but because of the avalanches that often roared from the peaks down the canyons of the Valsugana. (There are some who still remember a shoemaker, the father of a family, who was swept away in the Vallone delle Trappole. He was found in August by sheepdogs, with the sack containing his clogs still tied on his back.)

In short, in March of the year when our story begins, Tönle Bintarn was on his way home with a load of goods. At the first signs of habitation, the companions split up and took different paths so as not to be conspicuous, and he, at a confident but careful pace, came down the Platabech. His hobnails bit into the frozen snow, which remained firm in the stretches of shadow; in less than half an hour he would be home with his wife and children, to rest and sleep in a warm, dry bed. His wife and Petar, his oldest son, would later see about disposing of the goods.

When he heard "Halt!" he was more surprised than if they had fired a musket at him, but he didn't drop his load so as to be free to run. By now he was too close to home. He jumped down off the path, but the second revenue agent was waiting there below, and as he touched the ground he felt his arm being seized and the ritual cry: "Stop! We've got you!"

Then it was, when he felt the man's grasp on his arm, that he broke free and struck out blindly with his stick. The agent yelled and fell to the ground. He started running down through the woods where the daphne was already in bloom; he heard shots and the bullets chopping the beech twigs over his head, and then shouts—"Halt! Halt! Stop!"—and the crows cawing and a frightened blackbird, and then once again: "Halt! Stop, we know who you are!"

He stopped at a spot where he could observe without being seen. The two agents went down through the pastures; one was supporting his comrade, who with one hand held a handkerchief to his head. He saw them pause for a moment to talk to old Ballot, who was hoeing a patch of ground to sow lentils; they passed through the Grebazar meadows, stopped once more at the Pach, where they bathed and washed the head wound with running water, and finally set out toward the first houses in the town.

Then he ran down. He left his goods in the Spille sheep-fold and arrived home faster than ever. Hurriedly he explained to his wife and father what had happened, took something to eat, and went back to the woods to hide under a familiar shelf of rock.

An hour later, revenue agents and carabinieri under the command of an officer arrived at the hamlet. They searched the house thoroughly, of course, from cellar to hayloft, but found nothing but poverty. In the stable, where the floor had risen at least a meter from the fodder and manure of the winter, so that the muzzles of the sheep were at the level of the window and they could look longingly out at the Poltrecche pastures where the crocuses were already in bloom, a sergeant drove the six sheep and three lambs to one side in case the culprit might be hiding among them.

In the end, the lieutenant ordered all the inhabitants of the hamlet to assemble in front of the house. "One of the king's revenue agents has been seriously injured in the exercise of his duty," he said, with a Neapolitan accent. "We know who his attacker is, and so do you. If the criminal surrenders in the next few hours, we will show clemency. Otherwise . . . "—and he left the threat hanging by clenching his gloved hand in a fist. Then he went on: "You yourselves will be held accountable if you give him aid and shelter. Understand?"

No one said a word. Only one old man muttered something in a dialect that the others certainly did not understand. "Let's go!" the lieutenant ordered his men. And two abreast they marched back to the town along the narrow road with its stone markers. Dogs barked as they passed.

The fact that a revenue agent had been wounded by Tönle Bintarn became known in the district capital and all the surrounding communities with telephonic rapidity, though as yet there were no telephones. The police magistrate opened an investigation; the subprefect demanded a report from the chief of police and the commandants of the revenue corps and royal carabinieri. But most of all it was talked about in the shop of Puller, the barber and shoemaker, who gathered and circulated news and information for smugglers and policemen, state officials and innkeepers, storekeepers and quartermaster sergeants, woodcutters and herdsmen, hunters and priests.

The incident was likewise the subject of discussion, that same evening, in the officers' mess of the Sixty-third Alpine Company of the garrison. The young Piedmontese officers criticized the behavior and unsociable nature of these border people, and it was recalled that the famous Captain Casati had to intervene with a company of riflemen against about a hundred mountaineers who, without official authorization, had tried to cut timber in the woods of the Consortium. Who did these people think they were? But Lieutenant Magliano, who took care to report certain names to the royal conscription commission in order to have them assigned to his division, and recalling also that the attacker had been a sapper in his platoon when he, a second lieutenant fresh from military school, had been sent to our town, put an end to the discussion by inviting his messmates to join him in the chorus of a song that in those very days he had composed to an old popular tune. The words went: "On our caps we wear a trophy—of the royal house of Savoy—we wear it with faith and with joy—long live Italy and its rulers. / We'll scale the walls of Trent. . . . "

Another curious circumstance is that Tönle Bintarn, before being a sapper in the Alpine troops with Second Lieutenant Magliano, had also been a lance corporal in the Landwehr, at Budejovice in Bohemia, under the command of Major von Fabini. When after four years of service he was discharged and came home, our village had changed masters: instead of Franz Josef there was now Victor Emmanuel.

The day after the crime, Tönle's wife went into town with a dozen eggs and two kilos of sugar in her bag. Before crossing the Piazza della Fontana, she stopped at the Sterns' corner to take off her slippers and put on her shoes and stockings; then she tidied herself, walked across the piazza to a particular house, and climbed the stairs to the lawyer Bischofar's office.

Hearing her footsteps, the lawyer came out in the hall to usher her into his office, having first dismissed his little granddaughter, who had come to keep him company and dust the books and pictures, the portraits of Garibaldi on horseback and Mazzini with his hand on his broad forehead. As a student, or rather a seminarian, he had been at the siege of Venice in 1848 with Daniele Manin, and later with the "Free Corps" or Cimbrian Legion at the Vezzene pass to repulse Radetzky's Austrians and Croats.

"I know all about it," he told the woman once she was seated. "It's better that your husband not be seen around here for a good long time. Didn't he once work for a spell in the Styrian iron mines? He ought to go back there right away even if he hasn't been hired; he knows how to get there. And then he'll surely find a way to send you something to get along on; after all, it's better to be in an iron mine than in prison. From the way things look, and I've spoken to the magistrate about it, there's no chance of his getting off; maybe later, with time, there might be an occasion for an amnesty. Meanwhile, I'll try to get you something from the Charity Institute."

The lawyer Bischofar did not employ legalistic jargon; indeed, in talking to the local country people he used more words in the old dialect than in Venetian or Italian. He didn't accept the eggs or sugar, and in bidding her good-bye he asked her, since she had to pass through the hamlet of Chescie, to say hello to his friend Christian Sech.

The next night Tönle retraced his steps to the border. But to keep from being arrested, since they would certainly be on the lookout for him, he took a chance on the Val Caldiera Pass, descending by the Valon Porsig, where with the rough terrain and the danger of landslides, he was unlikely to encounter any agents.

Lower down, where the snow was soft, he had walked with snowshoes, but on the high slopes he needed to plant the points of his nailed shoes in the ice at every step. In the descent, the path had disappeared completely, and he had to follow the canyons, steadying himself on the snow with a stout stick and digging in his heels.

That same evening he was in Castelnovo and slept in a stable; next day he proceeded to Castel Tesin, where he knew the widow of an old fellow worker. There he would find a good bed and a plate of soup.

After they had talked about his mishap, and the jobs that weren't yet open, and how it wasn't right for him to stay in that house any longer than necessary, the widow offered to send him to her nephew, a print vendor, who would be leaving in a week for the Austrian lands with his box slung on his shoulder. He would have to go to Pieve to stock up on supplies from the printing houses, and would be able to buy some for him, too. The money she would advance him until he came back. She trusted him, and if he liked, so as not to feel indebted, he could later pay her 5 percent interest, as is customary among respectable folk.

Before accepting the proposal, he wanted to hear from the nephew how the situation really was, and went to his house.

Many times in the years he had been out in the world, first as a boy carrying water in the mines, then laying track for the railroads under construction, or even as a soldier, he had run across these rather odd itinerant peddlers who exhibited their wares at village fairs and festivals by hanging them from a string stretched under arcades or on the walls of churches; and they didn't sell things that were useful or necessary in a trade or for the house and fields, such as harnesses, hardware, utensils, buckles, cloth, and so on, but pieces of paper with pictures on them. Images of saints and illustrations that told stories that anyone, even illiterate people, could understand.

He, too, had lingered for an hour or so on Sundays to look at such pictures and read the captions, mulling over scenes from the Bible or ancient Rome, or of the Knights of the Round Table, or pictures of distant cities, costumes and countries, and Napoleon's wars.

He thought of this as he walked and reached the house, which lay some distance from Castel Tesin, in a meadow on the mountainside. He went in. There were lots of people inside, men and women of all ages, some around a large table, some next to the fireplace, some sitting on the stairs that led to the upper floor, and all of them were eating beans and polenta. He greeted everybody, wishing them good appetite, then said who he was and who he was looking for. A man left the fireplace and came forward. At first, with his round and rosy face, he looked like a kid, but his long, thick, red mustache showed he was over twenty.

They made room for him at the table, where a girl got up to give him her place; they asked him if he had eaten. He accepted a drop of grappa in a coffee cup. They talked.

Here, too, as at the widow's, he told his story and how he had had to leave home so as not to go to jail. Orlando, as the boy with the mustache was called, agreed to buy him the prints according to what he considered the demands of the market, but he also felt that after a certain period of apprenticeship it wouldn't be fair for them to compete in the same village squares. In short, he would start him off and then they would come to an agreement, perhaps to follow parallel routes and meet up in the evening, since Tönle didn't have a peddler's license and under the law would have to be his assistant.

They left next week, on foot. They had good shoes and good legs, and on their backs, slung by a leather strap, each carried a wooden box with a hundred or so prints lying flat and divided by subject and series.

These iconographic prints were the only art objects that for three centuries had spread the works of the great masters among countryfolk and the poorer classes in the cities, and in dwellings scattered across mountains and plains. The inhabitants of Tesino, old and expert itinerant peddlers—long ago they went around Europe hawking flint stones—had progressed to selling engravings from the famous Remondini printing house in Bassano Veneto all over the world: from Scandinavia to the Indies, Siberia to Peru. And all peoples and countries rightly had their own tastes. What appealed to the Lutherans of northern Europe was not acceptable to the Spaniards; the Russians wanted views of Paris or London or reproductions of Raphael, the French and the inhabitants of the Low Countries episodes from Napoleon's campaigns or costumes and landscapes from Muscovy or the Caucasus, the South Americans Madonnas of Guadalupe and Last Judgments, the Austrians romantic Italian landscapes and hunting scenes; and furthermore they all had their particular saints, some wanting a more elderly Saint Joseph or a younger Madonna.

Thus the print vendors had to be familiar with tastes and traditions, and suggest purchases to individual customers according to their age and sex, religious faith, the trade they pursued, and their passions. But it might also happen that in an isolated farmhouse in Galicia they wanted Raphael's *Marriage of the Virgin* or a *Pietà* by Michelangelo (these always sold better than the Flemish!), and in such cities as Vienna or Heidelberg an oleograph of Saint Anthony the Abbot, the one with the pig.

Tönle and his Valsugana partner traveled fast. At Bolzano, instead of taking the Isarco valley for the Brenner, they followed the course of the Adige. At Naturns they displayed their wares for the first time and sold enough to allow them to buy a few provisions of rye bread, smoked bacon fat, and cheese; then one of them stopped at Laces and the other proceeded to Schlanders, where they met up again that evening. They slept in a hayloft and then set out once more, with Tönle working the farms on the left side of the valley and the other those on the right. Three days later they rejoined each other at Glurns, where they spent the night in a stable inside the circle of the old walls, and next morning, at a fair that drew people from as far away as Valtellina and Switzerland, they did a brisk business. Then they took the road for the Resia Pass and entered the Vorarlberg.

They kept going for weeks, crossed the mountains, and at Landshut in Bavaria sold almost all their classical subjects. They therefore decided to head for Brno, where Giuseppe Pasqualini, himself from Castel Tesin, ran a modern printing shop for the mechanical reproduction of color prints by the oleographic method. There they would pick up a fresh supply and then proceed on their way. And besides, Pasqualini's prints allowed for a greater margin of profit, and were much in demand because people were charmed by their lively, natural colors and lifelike look.

As they approached Kraków, Orlando decided to cross the Carpathian mountains into Russian territory and try his luck by setting up shop in Kiev, or Moscow, or Saint Petersburg. He'd saved up a tidy sum and said that Tesino compatriots who had settled in those distant cities would help him. That evening, before parting, they ate and drank in an inn in

Kraków, where the Jewish proprietor asked to be paid not in money, but with a print showing the port of Amsterdam.

Alone, Tönle set out on the road back, but since he had neither a peddler's license nor a passport, only his discharge paper from the Landwehr, he had to avoid cities and towns. He resupplied himself with prints in Brno by sending another traveler from Tesino, whom he had met on the roads of Bohemia, to buy them. On his way through the villages in the provinces of Salzburg and the Tyrol, he sold all of them except two.

Cesare's dog didn't bark, but came to sniff his fustian trousers. It found many smells, all of them agreeable, and gently wagged its tail. Tönle noticed, without paying much attention, a row of diapers frozen stiff on the garden fence. He pulled the bolt of the latch, pushed the door, and entered without a word.

They hadn't been expecting him. He stood for a moment against the stone jamb and closed the door. His wife and his mother stopped spinning flax; his father, seated on a stool, was staring at him, having turned his gaze from the fire and taken the pipe from his mouth; Petar was the first to stand up in the corner under the lamp, where amid a pile of shavings he was smoothing pinewood staves with a knife. They came forward to greet him, the women embraced and kissed him; his father barred the door with the ash beam, then took him by the arm and drew him close to the fire in order to get a better look at him. There were so many things they all wanted to know, and the answers couldn't keep up with the questions. They went on telling and asking about all those months he had been away.

At the time when he had had to take to the hills his wife

had been pregnant scarcely two months and still hadn't known it, and now a little girl had been born. She had already been christened Giovanna; she was sleeping. There she lay on a sack of husks in her warm, dry cradle, sucking her thumb and ever so lightly breathing, once in a while puffing out her cheeks. Tönle had picked up the oil lamp, and holding it before him with his outstretched arm, stood and gazed at her: with no fear of showing his emotions, he forgot to bite the slice of polenta and the little piece of cheese that his mother had put in his hand.

He moved back to the fire, which Petar had stirred up by adding dry wood to give more heat and light. "They tried you in absentia," said the old man, "and sentenced you to four years. It's a good thing the revenue agent recovered in a little over a month. They wanted to give you seven years, but Bischofar the lawyer pleaded your case and even called Lieutenant Magliano to testify. You'd better not be seen around here because the police turn up now and then in the neighborhood; they've even come here to the house three or four times to find out if we knew where you were hiding."

He, on the other hand, wanted to know all about the birth, the potato and flax harvests, whether they had enough dry wood for the winter, how the sale of wool had gone, or if they'd kept it to spin and weave at home. He also wanted to know whether Petar had begun working with the shepherds or, since he'd seen him whittling wooden staves when he came in, if he hadn't gone over instead to the Prudeghar hamlet to learn the joiner's trade. No, they explained, he hadn't gone to the woodworking shop, but had started at home by himself, using his grandfather's tools; and besides at home there was firewood to be gathered and the crops to be seen to on the Moor; not to mention the sheep, which they hadn't sent to the Consortium's pastures with the other flocks, but kept down here on land leased by the community. Marco had started going to elementary school and every morning went down into town with the other children from the hamlet.

While they talked about these things, his wife kept looking at him as though trying to pierce through his clothing with her eyes; she had immediately laid aside her reel and spindle, and was holding his hand, squeezing it tightly. She was waiting for the moment when she could be alone with him and ask the things she couldn't ask in front of everyone else.

Tönle spoke without giving too many details; then, with a certain nonchalance, he took off his belt, unstitched it with his knife, and poured out in his hand the silver guldens that had been hidden inside.

"I earned them," he said, "by traveling through a lot of countries and selling prints."

He counted them in front of the whole family: there were thirty ringing pieces of twenty kreuzers each, a nice little sum, practically a fortune. He handed them to his wife. "Take these twenties," he said. "You can use them for the house."

From another hiding place he took ten more guldens, which he handed to his mother without saying a word.

Again he approached the cradle to gaze at little Giovanna, who was still asleep. He stretched out his hand to caress or awaken her, but drew back an inch or so from her reddened face. He thought he could see her smiling at him, and it brought a glow to his own face.

As he stepped back to the hearth, where the rest of the family was waiting for him to go on with his story, he remembered that before coming in he had left something outside the door. These were two prints, which he hadn't tried to sell because he liked them, and he wanted to have them framed and hung on either side of the fireplace. He unrolled them so that they could be seen by the light of the flames.

One was of a nighttime attack by a pack of wolves on a sleigh racing through a snowy forest. It was only with great difficulty and effort that the horses, maddened with terror, could be controlled by the driver, who had lost his fur cap and with his whip was trying to drive off a wolf that was about to sink its teeth into a horse. The eyes of other wolves could be seen glowing red amid the tree trunks, like lights in the darkness. In the back of the sleigh, a bearded man, kneeling on a heap of wares, was aiming a long rifle at the pursuing wolves. A reddish flash emerged from the rifle, splitting the darkness, and you could see the bullet entering the gaping jaws of a wolf that was about to leap on the sleigh. One beast was writhing on the ground, farther away another lay dead on the snow.

But the more you looked at it, the more you seemed to hear the whinnying of the horses, the crack of the whip, the howling of the wolves, the report of the rifle. They were all gripped by the story; at first they had gazed at the whole scene, then at all the details as Tönle pointed them out with his finger.

"But, Father," Marco asked him, "did they have wolves where you were?"

"I got as far as the Carpathian Mountains. They have them there, too. But they only attack sleighs in winter and when they're starving."

Silence fell and they all looked toward the door. They could hear a bitch outside barking at the moon, but it was a friendly sound.

Tönle spread out the second print: it showed a bear hunt. Against the background of a wooded mountain, a huge bear, upright on its hind legs, was fighting off a pack of dogs. Two dogs had their teeth in the bear, others were leaping around it, still others lay wounded on the grass, and there was blood on the grass, on the bear, and on the dogs. A bold-looking hunter brandished a long knife, while another aimed his rifle, waiting for the right moment to pull the trigger. An unarmed youth had picked up one of the dogs, its stomach torn and bleeding, and was carrying it away: his face as he gazed back open-mouthed at the bear expressed great astonishment and pity.

They admired this print, too, by the light of the fire, some remarking on the size of the bear, some on the courage of the dogs, others on the daring of the hunters.

"I'll make a couple of nice frames," Petar said finally. "I've got a piece of larch wood that shows the knots: they'll look great."

That night he could at last stretch out in his own bed, with his wife beside him and the two smallest children nearby in their cradles. He wasn't aware of the cold because their bodies quickly heated up. The ice had embroidered fantastic curtains on the windowpanes, and the moonlight reflected by the snow was suffused softly throughout the room, making a glittering pattern of frost on the walls, like so many stars spread across a mild sky. He made love to his woman several times and then fell asleep with one hand cupped on her breast.

He was awakened by the first light of dawn and the sound of festival bells, and by groups of people from the hamlets on their way to town singing a Christmas carol. The verses mingled in the frigid air, and he heard the song now loud, now faint; he couldn't hear the words even when he strained to listen, but from the direction and sound of the voices he was able to imagine: that would be the men from Ébene, those the women from the Bald and Prudeghar hamlets. He recalled how as a boy he, too, used to go singing along the roads—the snow would crunch under the hobnails of his shoes. He knew the words of the ancient carol by heart and sang along from memory:

Darnaach viärtansong iahr
as dar Adam hat gavêlt
ist kemmet af disa belt
dar ûnzar libe Gott . . .
. . . .
Gabüart in bintar zait
in armakot, un vrise
z'öxle alloan, mit plise,
un z'esele haltenz barm . . .

Oh Gott ba d'allez môghet!
Von eüch beghen ist hûmmel
d'earda, dar gliz, dar tümmel
un Iart gabûart so arm! . . .

(Four thousand years
after Adam sinned,
our beloved God
came into this world . . .
. . . .
Born in wintertime,
in misery and cold,
only an ox with its breath
and an ass kept him warm . . .

O God who can do everything!
Because of you there's the sky,

19

the earth, the lightning, the thunder,
and you were born so poor!)

The bells had stopped. His wife rose and hurriedly got
dressed to go down and light the fire, as she did on all other
mornings of the year. He heard Petar talking in a low voice,
then opening and closing the door, and voices under the windows: boys and girls calling each other. And then singing:

> Gasegt an stearn in hûmmel,
> drai mann von morgond lantar
> in könighe gaväntar
> leghensich af an bek . . .

> (Having seen a star in the sky,
> three men from the East
> in regal robes
> set out on the road . . .)

"But why do those kids start with that verse when it comes
near the end?" he said. And got up.

Three months of patient waiting began for him: he couldn't
show his face during the day, and to go into town was out of
the question. Sometimes in the evening after supper he
would go as far as the Nappas' stable, where the men of the
hamlet met to shoot the breeze. They talked about their work
experiences, about the seasons, about encounters they'd had
in the outside world, the customs of people, the character of
foreign women. But even the inhabitants of the plain below
our mountains were looked on as foreigners!

Some had worked on the railroads and gone all the way to
Anatolia, and they told how in order to defend themselves
from wolves they'd had to build bonfires at night along the

edge of their barracks, and how they'd had to be guarded on the job by soldiers against raids by Bulgarian and Macedonian bandits.

Sometimes, under their breath, they sang the song of the *eisenponnar*—the construction workers who leveled mountains and flung bridges across rivers to make way for the railroad:

> —And mornings at dawn
> you hear the trumpets play;
> the *eisenponnar* are going away,
> so long, sweetheart, want to come?

And the women, who were spinning, answered sweetly:

> —Yes of course I'd come.
> But where will you take me?
> —I'd take you over the sea
> to an *eisenponnar*'s fine house.
> —Over the sea
> that's far from home;
> but though I die of homesickness
> I won't let you go away alone.

Softly and submissively, the song told itself, like beads on a rosary, while the spindles and reels buzzed like bees and stirred the warm air in the stable as though it were springtime.

This song was always followed by a silent pause, until someone who had been in Hungary starting talking about the excavation work there on the endless irrigation canals and the Decauville wagons drawn by coupled teams of horses. But they'd been lucky in Hungary to have horses drawing the wagons, because in Germany, with its Kaiser, the wagons in the caves and mines had to be pushed by hand!

Tönle didn't always sleep in his bed; when he came home in the evening he would climb up the ladder to the hayloft: should the police pay a visit, he could easily reach the woods from the back of the house. Sometimes, when a warning came from Puller's shop, he went up to the Pûnes' hut, where he had made a soft berth for himself in the hay. On nights of heavy snow, when the police were unlikely to go around searching for him, he dared to sleep in his own bed with sheets and his wife.

It so happened that one sunny afternoon, after the men of the hamlet had performed the thankless task of shoveling the roads leading to the town, three policemen and a sergeant had come to the house looking for him. (Had they heard something indicating his presence?) Luckily Marinle Ballot had seen them coming, and picking up her copper pails, had walked quickly to Prunnele and from there to the Bintarn house to warn them. Tönle had time to slip out the back door, take the logging trail, and go and hide in the woods, under the usual shelf of rock, where neither the snow nor the police ever came, and from where he could watch without being seen. The children said nothing, nor did the other inhabitants of the hamlet.

The carabinieri kept coming, and one night they made everybody get out of bed and ransacked the house as they had the first time.

But by now winter was almost over; the days were getting longer and the finches were starting to rehearse their first love songs and the crossbills to build their nests. The sun was strong enough to melt the snow on the roofs, and the thatch dripped water that in the night created festoons of shining icicles along the southern eaves.

On the last three evenings in February, in accordance with

22

tradition, the children went out to summon the spring with bells: by now they, too, were tired of snow, long evenings, and being shut up in the house, and like the birds and the roebucks they looked forward to long days with the sun high and green grass. Looking at the pile of ashes on the hearth and the reduced supply of wood, the old people remarked, "Another winter gone by," and after sunset went outside to watch the bonfires on top of the Moor and the Spilleche: it was these fires that burned up the winter and showed migratory birds which way was north. They listened joyfully to the children who ran barefoot through the meadows still covered with patches of snow and along the paths connecting the houses, singing:

> Scella, scella mearzo,
> snea dehin,
> gras dehear
> alle de dillen lear.
> Az der kucko kuck
> pluut der balt;
> ber lange lebet
> sterbet alt!

> (Ring, ring, March,
> away with the snow,
> here's the grass,
> all the haylofts are empty.
> When the cuckoo sings
> the woods bloom;
> if you live a long time
> you die old.)

When the titlarks started singing over the sunny terraced slopes, he again left home and crossed the border. Though he would have liked to go back to selling prints in the territories of the Habsburg Empire, he was unable to do so this time: his

Valsugana friend had not come home that winter and there was no telling where he'd ended up, maybe in Kraków or Kiev, and since Tönle was not one of Franz Josef's subjects, they refused him an itinerant peddler's permit even when he showed his discharge paper from the Landwehr regiment to the Austrian police commissioner in Borgo. He didn't even have a passport, nor any recent job offer; they stamped an old work card for him and let it go at that.

The first months of spring, the hardest, were spent stripping timber in the Carinthian forests and working for a while with the peasants of Styria, and once he had a little money he made his way across Burgenland and arrived in Hungary, where he finally signed a contract until December with a horse trainer for the army.

It was an immense plain, where the outer limits of the pastures were marked by canals and rivers; in the middle of the stud farm was a village with scattered trees and spacious stables, drinking troughs, and kitchen gardens with pumpkins and cabbages. He and a few others had to watch over the horses in the pasture, cut and dry the hay, take care of the stables, the smithy, and the fodder supply. In late September the imperial remount commission and a cavalry inspector arrived in the village.

They rounded up the horses in a large paddock and the selection lasted from Monday to Saturday: stallions and brood mares, males and females to be broken in, colts to be allowed to grow, and some to be eliminated because they were sick or defective. The commission's veterinarian had also been asked to find a pacer for a Hungarian army colonel, and Tönle, who during these months had acquired a certain knack, had spotted a truly beautiful sorrel, which earned him praise and a good tip, allowing him that same Saturday evening at the end of work to celebrate in high spirits. In these villages, at the end of every work cycle or season, a gypsy orchestra always turned up playing the czardas.

All in all it was a good season, not so much for the pay, which was rather low, but for work that he liked, and for the festivities and dances on Saturday, the company, and the good beer.

On the way home that year, he stopped in Austria with a family of peasants, where he had worked planting potatoes, and in view of the exceptional abundance and quality of the harvest, he asked for some ten kilos to take back with him for planting. These potatoes had smooth dark skins, verging on violet, and were firm and white inside, and though not the very best, the peasants assured him, they had the merit of ripening slowly and withstanding frost: in other words, they didn't sprout buds in the spring and could very well last from one harvest to another.

That Christmas eve he arrived home with only a few silver guldens but with a kind of potato that year after year was to produce good harvests and spread throughout our mountains.

2

Time went by and one year he found himself in Prague, where he remembered having heard that a compatriot of his named Andrea Raconat, the son of his relative Catina Pûne, had become an official of the empress Maria Anna Carolina, wife of Ferdinand of Austria, the former king of Lombardy-Venetia, and that she had named him superintendent of the imperial wine cellars. In the city he asked the gendarmes, and since Andrea Raconat had married the eldest daughter of the chief magistrate Sabotka, it was not hard to find the building where he lived.

He was warmly welcomed, and his fellow countryman, who had never been back to our little homeland since 1866, and had had news of it only from letters or what he had read in the newspapers, had many questions to ask about his relatives, friends, neighbors, the public authorities and the government, the town notables. He also invited him to supper, in his home with his wife and children, and even after all these years this official showed emotion and nostalgia in speaking the old language and hearing words and names he thought he'd forgotten forever. His family looked at him in amazement: never had they seen him so talkative and excited.

When supper was over, the two of them withdrew to the

study. Andrea Raconat called for two bottles of wine, and they talked at length about their childhood.

Thus it was that our fellow countryman and his distant relative got him a good job as a gardener at the Hradcany Castle in Malá Strana. It could have been a steady, full-time job, as we'd say today, but when the first snow fell on the roofs and gardens of Prague, he felt an urgent need to return home. Not for nothing in our old language does *bintarn* mean "hibernator."

And he was gripped by a great feeling of homesickness, homesickness for that puny wild cherry tree on the roof and for all that lay beneath the four thatched slopes. Just as there were forces that drove him to leave in the spring, so there were those that made him go back at the end of autumn, forces stronger than willpower, like the rotation of the seasons, the migrations of birds, sunrise and sunset, the phases of the moon.

He finished up his work: he covered the rose beds with dry leaves, cut back the stems of the perennials, dug up the dahlia bulbs and stored them in the cellar, covered the fertilizer in the flower beds, raked the paths. He said good-bye to the head gardener and the castle superintendent, and went down into the city to take leave of his fellow countryman.

Once again, on that December evening, the superintendent of the imperial wine cellars kept him to supper with his family, and later, as they said good-bye, his face expressed a profound nostalgia. "Say hello to all my mother's relatives," he urged him, "and our hamlet, and the Moor." These words contained the happy games of childhood and youth, the bonfires of spring, the hunt for birds' nests in the woods, and sled races on the ice.

Tönle set out on his homeward journey, and since he was late and had plenty of money, instead of going on foot this time, to speed up the trip he took the train from Prague, which in only three days landed him in Trent.

Under a full moon in December and taking the smugglers' route, where the snow had not yet piled too high, he crossed the border, walked for four hours, and once again saw the cherry tree on the roof.

His old mother had died in September, on the feast day of Saint Matthew; and he recalled how on that very day, the twenty-first, he had been overcome by a strange feeling of apprehension, a sort of melancholy uneasiness, wanting to be by himself in the castle park among the tall trees, which were beginning to turn red, and with no desire to eat or drink: like that mild anxiety that sometimes overtakes animals, too.

The seasons passed and came round: from the melting of the snow until it fell again he journeyed through Habsburg lands and towns, working wherever he could, sometimes with good results, sometimes not. In winter he was holed up at home, either in the hamlet, or in the forest to cut firewood, or in some hut where he wouldn't be caught by the police, who had every intention of arresting him and making him serve his four-year prison sentence. But always, at the beginning of winter around Christmas, he returned home in the early hours of the night, or rather when the cherry tree on the thatched roof had faded in the dusk. And as he crossed the threshold of his house he would find a new son or daughter. The clerks at the registry office had ironical things to say about issuing birth certificates in his name, but the parish priest cut them short: if the king's policemen were unable to arrest the father, said to be on the run across the frontier, that didn't mean that his wife hadn't conceived by him!

Meanwhile, time left its mark on the faces of his family and friends, new things were happening and new ideas circulating even among our rural folk. By now there were many who went to work outside the borders of Italy; groups of them left in the spring, with the tools of their trade in a wheelbarrow, setting out on foot by the Asstal and the Menador as far as Trent, where those who could afford it might even take the train. Sometimes these groups included boys just out of elementary school, and at the border the guards on both sides let them go through without observing the formalities, at most asking if they had their baptismal certificates in their pockets.

But those who were able, by first working in Prussia or Austria-Hungary, to save enough money for their passage emigrated to the Americas. Over there, they wrote, things were quite different: there was always work and the pay was better than in any other country.

People were beginning to talk about socialism, workers' associations, artisans' cooperatives. Anyone lacking the courage to utter the word "socialism" said and wrote "sociality," but, oddly enough, those who made use of communal property, that is to say, all the residents of our communes, were called "communists" even in official documents.

Even in our part of the world, where for centuries those responsible for the public weal had been chosen by the people, two parties emerged that under the designation of progressives and moderates disguised the interests of a few leading families: thus what had never happened in eight hundred years of free government now took place. Discord, dissension, lawsuits, flights abroad; priests and professional men were involved, proletarians and artisans; and there were those who sold votes and those who made money on the emigrants. We owe the documentation of this hectic period to a few issues of a small weekly newspaper, costing ten centesimi, and written and printed almost entirely by an elementary schoolteacher, who, because of the things he had written, had to depart one fine day for Argentina on the steamship *Sirio* of the Florio-Rubattino line.

While the moderate side founded the Savings and Loan Association, the progressives founded the Workers' Association. While one side had a brass band with red caps, the other had one with green caps and pheasant feathers; and while one side played for Garibaldi or the Porta Pia and the end of papal rule in Rome, the others played for the Piedmontese Constitution or the birthday of Queen Margherita.

Coinciding with the decline in home spinning and weaving (large factories had been set up in Schio), a cottage industry sprang up for the manufacture of wooden boxes to hold medicines and perfumes, in which children and girls between the ages of ten and fifteen could earn, in ten hours, an average of sixty centesimi a day.

The independent newspaper I mentioned also received letters like these (surely corrected by the editor): "I work in a mine with some of my countrymen, the most productive mine in all of Prussia and maybe in all of Europe. Almost eight hundred men have been working under this hill. It's a good job but pretty dangerous, since I don't have eyes in the back of my head to keep me out of harm's way. . . . At four o'clock in the morning I must get started and walk for as many as forty minutes deep inside the mountain: before get-

ting to work I have to do 2300 meters starting at its foot. . . .
And for ten hours I have to stay there, and then I come out
weak and exhausted from working too hard and from the bad
air you have to breathe down there. You see so many young
fellows between twenty and thirty who look like they're fifty!
Almost all the ones who work down here. Besides the bad air
there's something else that's not good for your health: the
lamp, which gives off smoke when you light it, and it all goes
into your stomach, and if you don't cough it up you must get
out of there or die. Thank God, I get rid of it, so do my compatriots; but you see a lot of men ruined by it. . . . " And
another miner from Algringen writes: "I work about a thousand meters inside the mountain. At five o'clock I leave home
praying to God to keep me out of danger. I go in the tunnel
and work hard all day until five or six in the afternoon. Then
I go back to the barracks quite satisfied if I've earned five lire
in the course of the day, sometimes more and sometimes
less. . . . "

In winter, at the taverns in the center of town, miners and
railway workers discussed these things and drank wine. Tönle
Bintarn, who of course couldn't show his face among them,
stayed holed up in the hamlet, and there were evenings in the
stables when he spoke in a low voice about the *Communist
Manifesto,* which he had read in German the year he had
worked in the mines of Hayngen.

Also in those years it turned out that certain well-off indi-
viduals, not yet rich but certainly smart, sided with the Red
Caps, the workers' party, in urging the people to take all the
old communal property—woods, pastures, and arable land—
and divide it up per capita. The aim of the instigators was
obvious: once the great common patrimony had been split

up this way, it would be easy to buy the property once held by the community from the starving emigrant proletarians, and for a miserable price in staples—barley, flour, cheese. These phony progressives who supported the Red Caps were opposed by the "mauves"—conservatives who accepted such signs of progress as universal education, the telegraph, and public lighting, but also looked with fear and distrust on the restlessness of the poorer classes. But between the two of them, the ones who really prospered were the entrepreneurs contracting to build military fortifications.

Meanwhile, the new century, the twentieth, had come, and there was a great celebration in the town. The volunteer firemen had all been mobilized at their headquarters in Vitadoro, and after polishing their ladders, pumps, nozzles, and hoses, and making sure everything worked, they turned out in full uniform. That afternoon they arrived in the center of town preceded by joyous troops of boys and girls, the jingle of harness bells, and the hoofbeats of the six showy horses that drew the fire trucks. To the trills, long and short, of the mustachioed commander's whistle, and his commands curt as whiplashes, the volunteers sprang to fit nozzles to hoses, to try the hand pumps that drew water from the Pach, and finally, amid the great admiration of the spectators and the trepidation of the girls, they lifted their long flexible ladders and leaned them against the tallest houses in the center of town, since it was feared that the fireworks to be set off on the Gaiga in the middle of the night might ignite thatched and wooden roofs and destroy everything. When, along with all the comments, the oohs and ahs, and cries of careful!, the test was over, they all went to the Stone Marten Inn, where the mayor ordered wine all around.

The first to arrive was the military band of the Alpine troops, right after their five o'clock mess, and all the children who lined up to wait at the main door for leftovers from that day's "special meal" beat time to the march on hastily washed tins. Next came the Red Caps' band, but the musicians were already playing cheerfully out of tune: they had started out from one end of our long town, stopping to wet their whistles at every inn along the way, and now it was hard to get their lips back on the mouthpieces of their instruments. The Civic Band, however, and the Banda Mora put on a serious program, playing Verdi and Puccini, with duets by those two chief wind instruments, tenor and soprano, who volleyed the tune back and forth from one window to another of two houses on opposite sides of the square. And the people applauded and demanded encores from the two performers with such powerful lungs.

Gangs of boys were having fun throwing snowballs even at the policeman Frello, who already stank of liquor since early morning; while the girls, albeit with much shrieking, simpering, and giggling, went so far as to put handfuls of snow down the necks of young lads, who comported themselves manfully for the occasion.

From the Trattoria alla Torre to the Caffè al Mondo, the Imperial Eagle, the Alpine Club, the White Cross, and through all the taverns there was a happy mingling of people, calling on one another, each inviting others to eat and drink, such as had never happened at any other celebration.

At midnight, during the solemn mass, the Schola Cantorum of the parish sang the chorale by Maestro Perosi "*Al Signor levate, O gente . . . ,*" and then, when all the people and the authorities and officials and the Alpine soldiers of the garrison had poured back into the streets and squares, the signal was given to launch, from the top of the Gaiga, the great fireworks display that scared all the dogs for miles around and the tomtits, bullfinches, and thrushes in the houses of bird catchers.

But Tönle was unable to join his friends and neighbors. Why should he get himself arrested on this very night of merrymaking? And why should he be the only one not to participate in the celebration that had been so often discussed in the twilight of long evenings amid the hum of reels and spindles? In the afternoon he had climbed up Mount Katz, then from the Gharto woods he had dragged over the snow, a little below the cross, a big pile of dead branches cut from standing trees, and seated on a log in front of the Runzes' hut, he waited for the great event. From up there he heard the bands playing full blast and the clamor of the people. After the phantasmagoria of the fireworks, and once the echoes had faded over the mountains and the dogs stopped barking, he lighted his lone fire and took a sip of grappa from a small bottle that he had brought with him. More than one person in town saw his fire, and the folks from our hamlet, who had gone down to celebrate with everyone else, winked happily at each other.

But just as he was unable to spend the famous night of 1900 with all the other people and his family, so a few months later he couldn't celebrate the marriage of one of his daughters to a Camplàn in the Bôrtoni hamlet. The wedding feast included fresh bread, chocolate, milk, and even veal stew with polenta (but this dish was only for the adults). He had given her in marriage with a small dowry of silver thalers, and the trousseau had all been spun and woven in the house at no small sacrifice, since the bolts of cloth, instead of being taken to the Sterns and exchanged for other goods, had been stored for three winters in the chests at home.

It was in 1904 that our Bintarn was at last able to show his face in the streets and fields and woods without fear of being arrested by the police or the carabinieri. In that year the crown prince was born to the royal family, and for the occasion an amnesty and pardon were granted.

The lawyer Bischofar handled the matter with dispatch and through influential friends was able in a short time to bring it to a successful conclusion. What a relief, finally! Our Tönle's wife immediately took the lawyer a dozen fresh eggs and a bag of field dandelions. "Besides," she said, "when my husband returns for the winter, he'll come and repay you in some way."

To tell the truth, he was getting a little too old by now to go wandering about the world looking for work. The boys had grown up, and three of them were employed on the fortifications that the state was building along the border, facing the ones that Marshal Conrad was already completing on the other side. With the Hinterknotto defensive barracks long since finished, where a garrison of Alpine troops from the Bassano battalion was stationed, as well as the Rasta and Laita fortifications, work had begun on the large forts at the Lisser, Verena, and Campolongo Passes. But for all the sappers and carpenters and unskilled laborers employed on these projects, there were still as many countrymen who chose to cross the Tyrolean Alps in the spring, and just as many embarking on the ocean voyage to Australia or the Americas.

Bintarn, who had enlarged his little flock with his savings from so many odd jobs over the years, took his forty sheep to pasture from May to October, sometimes running afoul of the forest rangers when he surreptitiously let his animals trespass on some clearing in the communal woods; given his previous record, he had to be especially careful not to get himself reported, but most of the time the rangers who knew about it looked the other way.

Roving with his flock, he often ran into Doctor Paul, E. von Paul, an Austrian scientist with an interest in botany, geology, languages, and history, who used to come and spend his summers in our town, taking lodgings in a hotel in the center where government clerks and officers in the Italian army also stayed.

Everyone knew and respected Dr. Paul, who would hike tirelessly over our mountains, and whenever he met Bintarn, would stop and talk to him with an air of kindly interest. Indeed, if he heard that he was somewhere in the neighborhood, he went looking for him and asked him to speak, not in German or Czech or Venetian, but in our very old dialect, even though there were many words he not only didn't know and had to ask to have translated into some other language, but whose origin he wasn't even able to discover. There were so many of these obscure words that Dr. Paul was amazed. But this scholar was also interested in knowing the exact location of the very few springs in our mountains (a limestone base does not retain water on the surface, and our karstic mountains are like a sieve, while the large springs lie below at the foot of the broad terraces, in the Valsugana or the Veneto Plain). Dr. Paul also wanted to discover and explore paths and mule tracks; he went hiking every day with his knapsack and alpenstock, and sometimes he got lost in the maze of charcoal burners' paths that branched out through the tangles of mountain pine.

One day in September 1913, as the herds from the Vezzene were crossing the border on their return to Italy and descending once more to the plain, Dr. E. von Paul, who by his amiability had made so many friends among our countrymen and officials, crossed the frontier in the other direction to return to Austria. He was accompanied as far as the customs barrier by his friend Nicola Parènt, master woodcarver of rare skill and a peaceful man if ever there was one. After drinking a bottle of pilsner at the Terminus Inn under the eyes of the border guards, they parted effusively.

Some time later, the rumor spread in town that the cordial and likable Dr. Paul was actually an officer in the Austro-Hungarian artillery, and that his apparently harmless knapsack contained sketches and photographs of fortifications, mountains, roads, and springs.

THREE

On 28 June 1914 came the pistol shots in Sarajevo, but Tönle heard the news from a charcoal burner more than a month after the event. He was with his sheep on the Zingarellenbeck and the charcoal burner was on his way to cut mountain pine near the Goat Cave; they had stopped at the springlet to drink the fresh water that issued from between the layers of rock.

"I heard down in the village, at the Stone Marten Inn," said the charcoal burner, "that they've killed Francesco Giuseppe's son in Serbia. War is supposed to have broken out with Russia and France."

"Franz Josef's son?" asked Tönle. "But he died at Mayerling in '89, I was on my way to a job in those parts, I remember, and his name was Rudolf. Maybe they've killed the archduke, Franz Ferdinand, the heir to the throne."

"Yes, that's the one," confirmed the charcoal burner. "With his wife, they said at the inn."

Tönle, though he'd never gone to school, had learned to read and reckon with figures as needed, he could make himself understood in three or four languages, and besides he had always had a passion for history, at least for the history of those countries where every year he was driven to go by the need to make a living, and on sleepless nights in Hungary or

Austria or Bohemia, Bavaria, Silesia, or Galicia, he had learned many things by listening. He explained to the charcoal burner: "It must have been Austria-Hungary that declared war on Serbia, which means that Russia, because of the Balkan question, will have declared war on Austria-Hungary; so Germany then will go to war with Russia, and France with Germany. But we're in the Triple Alliance with Austria and Germany. . . . " He said all this while the sheep grazed on fresh grass, water flowed from the fissures in the rock, and the blackbirds fluttered among the pines.

When the charcoal burner had gone on his way up the Snealoch path, he sat down on a stone in the sun and lit his pipe. But if his eyes were watching the sheep, his thoughts were elsewhere. He remembered how, many years before, at the Budejovice barracks he had marched in formation under the eyes of Major von Fabini, and then again, when there was a change of government, at the Paloni barracks in Verona, again marching in formation under the eyes of Colonel—and Cavaliere—Nicola Heusch.

But how strange, he thought, in Austria I had a commander with an Italian name and in Italy a commander with an Austrian name. But then, smoking his pipe and thinking further, he concluded that it wasn't at all strange; the rich, whether in Italy or Austria, are always the rich, and for poor people it makes no difference whether they're ordered around by one or the other. It had always been up to them to work, to be soldiers, and even to die in wars. But maybe the proletarian revolution will happen in Germany, as Marx had explained in the *Manifesto* he had read with the miners. What year was that? Maybe 1890. Certainly they wouldn't call him up in the war. Who then? Von Fabini or Cavaliere Heusch? His sons, the ones who had stayed at home, they'd be called up for sure. In the distance he saw a line of Alpine troops moving slowly along the crest of the Kempel; among them would be his son Matío, who had been conscripted into the Bassano battalion.

That summer, not only did the Alpine troops of the garrison carry out maneuvers in our mountains with horse-drawn gun carriages, but other detachments as well, though not all that many. Troop encampments were set up along the edges of the woods, field kitchens gave off smoke, every day the fusiliers held target practice at the Petareitle rifle range, and sappers marked the hits. But women and girls, when they went to gather firewood or work on the plots of land, always stayed in a group, because, they said, the Neapolitan soldiers (and by this they meant all soldiers from Tuscany on down) were rather aggressive. But since it's true that people are the same all over, there were even some women who went looking for the army camps at night. A lot of money also circulated, because supplying the soldiers, the return of many railway workers due to the war, the building of roads and fortifications, the laundries, and all the business deals and exchanges had created something like a general euphoria. The inns, the hotels with electricity, and the Eden movie theater were always crowded, and until late at night, or early morning, depending on your point of view, you heard singing and shouting, laughing and squabbling, while against this general euphoria and moral degradation, the old white-haired parish priest, he who in 1848 had fought against the Austrians, hurled anathemas from the pulpit.

But Tönle Bintarn was grazing his sheep outside all this; often, in his solitude, thoughts crossed his mind of what the charcoal burner had told him and what life had taught him;

and perhaps he was able to see the things and events that were happening in a vast historical panorama—solitude, the mountains?—that may have escaped most people because they were submerged in them.

One day, when he was on the Boalgrüne with his flock, he saw a detachment of soldiers coming up toward him who even from a distance started yelling and waving in his direction. He did not budge from where he was, and only got to his feet the better to observe them. They marched through the sheep, while the dog, the fur on its neck bristling, growled menacingly. He called it to heel in an undertone and waited unperturbed.

The officer came up at the head of the patrol, sweating and with his jacket unbuttoned at the neck where he wore the white regulation stripe. Standing there in front of Tönle, he took off his cap and mopped his forehead. From his insignia Tönle saw that he was a lieutenant in the field artillery. The soldiers were standing around him in silence, and Tönle waited for him to speak. Finally the officer told him that tomorrow he would have to clear out with his sheep and go down to the Dhorbellele woods, because they were going to fire projectiles from up here.

To Tönle's remark that grazing was forbidden in the Dhorbellele woods, the lieutenant replied that they had already reached an agreement with the forest rangers and the mayor and so he needn't worry about it. Tönle muttered something to himself, the expression of a thought, the conviction of something imminent and unavoidable: if they were going to allow sheep to graze in a forbidden wood while the soldiers fired their cannons over the grazing lands, everything was topsy-turvy, and if these things were being done here on the border with Austria, with whom Italy was allied, one could only conclude that they were getting ready for stormy times. He muttered all this in a language incomprehensible to them, and one of them said out loud, "But what's this old yokel talking about?" The lieutenant may have wanted to add something, but Tönle's harsh and ironical look stopped him.

The soldiers stayed with him for half an hour and ate bread and tinned meat. The lieutenant asked if he'd sell him a lamb for the officers' mess, to which he replied that lambs were born to grow up and bring forth more lambs and give wool, not to be eaten by officers. One soldier, who so far had kept silent, waited until the others were leaving before asking him about the sheep: how many did he have and how many lambs, how long would he stay here on these pastures that were so high up but where the grass was good, and when would the snow fall? Then he observed that these sheep were bigger and fatter than the ones where he came from, that their wool was thicker, and their teats less developed. Didn't he milk them? To Tönle's replies he said that he, too, was a shepherd in his own country, across the sea in Sardinia, and that he didn't like being a soldier.

Meanwhile, his comrades had halted down below and were yelling for him to come, whereupon he said good-bye to the old man with a nod of his head, almost a bow, and ran down toward the valley.

He heard one day that the war had begun from two townsmen, Stefano and Toni Haus, who had come up to hunt for grouse. He knew them both well, because every autumn for years they had come looking for him to ask where the birds were nesting, and they always took the opportunity to smoke their pipes together and exchange a few words.

And, besides, they weren't like those Venetian counts who went hunting wearing white cotton gloves and with a Negro servant to carry their knapsack and rifle: the rifle would be handed to them when the dogs were already pointing, and as soon as they'd fired they handed it back to the servant. He had seen them doing this many times and didn't much like it, and so he tried to steer clear of them, even though once when it started snowing and they took shelter in his lean-to, they wanted to leave him two silver lire to pay for the firewood they'd used up.

It was still early morning when Stefano and Toni Haus came upon him at the Bisen-Stoan Pass, and he had lit a fire to reheat some polenta for a snack. They told him that Austria had declared war on Serbia, and Russia on Austria, and Germany on Russia, and France and England on Germany. In short, all Europe was in an uproar, and almost every day in town a lot of men were being called to arms.

Tönle listened in silence: he was thinking of his conversation with the charcoal burner and with the artillery lieutenant; he thought of his sons, of the Sardinian shepherd, and of many others he had met while working beyond the borders.

Stefano and Toni, having asked permission, put their own polenta on the coals. They talked about game, and asked where he had last seen grouse and ptarmigans flying up. They ate; they took the pig bladders with their shag tobacco out of their pockets and smoked their pipes in silence; they took a drink of water.

Tönle knocked the bowl of his pipe against the palm of his hand and pointed his stick at a clearing in the pines where two or three of the year's young grouse had flown up, then at the bare summit of stones and yellow grass where he had seen ptarmigans feeding.

Then, as though following a deep-seated thought, he said, "Maybe the governments are going to war because they're afraid the people will wake up and become too strong."

"The newspapers are saying," Stefano replied, "that we must liberate Trent and Trieste and our brothers beyond the frontier."

Tönle gazed beyond the line of mountains that marked the border and at his sheep peacefully grazing, then shook his head, replying only, "*Mah.*"

They said good-bye, promising to meet over a plate of tripe soup at the Imperial Eagle on the feast day of Saint Matthew.

For centuries it has been the tradition on 21 September for shepherds and herdsmen, charcoal burners and woodcutters to get together to celebrate, and after the solemn mass to go in cheerful groups to the inns, there to buy and sell in preparation for the winter, and to make an assessment of the season just past and a forecast for the one to come. But that year, 1914, they spoke not so much of business as of the war and the news that arrived in town every day with the newspapers. In Puller's shop there was less talk of smuggling and revenue agents than of the Balkans, the Dardanelles, Germany, Russia, Belgium, and often the names of cities came up where our miners and tracklayers had gone to work.

Tönle Bintarn had moved his sheep down to the community pastures; he had sheared them in the Gharto farmyard, and on the day of the feast he negotiated the price of the wool with the dealers and made more money than he would ever have expected. But this didn't strike him as a good sign, since when money is plentiful it's not worth all that much. So that evening—he had always treated himself to the evening of 21

September, even when he was in the outside world and couldn't go home—he had drunk a couple of extra glasses of red wine and was swaying from one side of the road to the other with the dog, who ran ahead of him and every so often stopped to wait; he also met a few off-duty soldiers who shouted jokingly at him. At the Grebazar hamlet he was overtaken by Bepi Pûn, a shepherd boy who had spent his season's pay at the fair for a pair of leather shoes with sturdy soles, and was proudly carrying them suspended by the laces around his neck.

They walked on together, and Bepi heard Tönle deliver some strange soliloquies about the war, the price of wool, soldiers, the castle in Prague, Rudolf of Habsburg, the prints he had once peddled, Hungarian horses, and all in happy confusion. Every so often he stopped in the middle of the road and, leaning on his long shepherd's stick, ended each muddled thought with: "By Jesus, I've seen lots of things in my life, but you, *maindar kindar,* you're going to see a lot more!"

He arrived home, and as he entered the kitchen where wood was burning in the fireplace but the lamp had not yet been lit, he noticed immediately that his wife was not there to greet him, and his chest was gripped by anxiety and a sad presentiment, while the effect of the wine he had drunk at the fair instantly wore off. It was not his wife who was stirring the bronze cooking pot, as he had always seen her do after his mother's death, but his daughter-in-law, and his grandchildren were silently watching the fire. Nor was his son Petar there, smoking his pipe after having seen to the animals. He went over to the fire and looked at his daughter-in-law in silence, questioning her with his eyes, and she answered him with a nod of her head as though to say, "She's upstairs in the bedroom."

He rushed up the wooden stairs; on the landing the bedroom door stood wide open, and an oil lamp hung over the bed from a ceiling beam. His wife was lying in the big pinewood bed, and she looked so small and shrunken, she could hardly breathe, and her face was all shriveled. Petar stood motionless at the foot of the bed.

He took one of her hands in his, it was dry and cold, the veins on the back hard and distended. She opened her eyes and tried to smile at him. Petar said, "I sent Carlo for the doctor. You didn't run into him on the way? After we came back from the fair, she wanted us to go up the Moor and get some potatoes. When the sun had gone down she didn't feel well, and I carried her home piggyback. She says she's cold. Brigida put a hot brick at her feet."

Tönle nodded his head and had the chair brought closer. He sat there immobile, watching her and holding her cold hands; her eyes were half-closed; her nose seemed to have become ever so much thinner, and the wrinkles in her face smaller and more numerous. Her cheeks were sunken, the sunburnt color of her skin was taking on an ashen look, and her hair, drawn back at the nape of her neck and held with a bone comb, was perhaps bothering her because she freed one hand from Tönle's and tried to loosen it. Tönle gently raised her a little on the pillow.

The whole house had become silent, the children kept still, and the daughter-in-law moved about the kitchen without making any noise; even from the bedroom one could hear the crackle of flames in the fireplace. Tönle went on gazing at that face and at the hands now resting on the blanket, and he became aware of the time and lives that had gone by: his wife's, his own, those of his old parents, of his children, and even those that would go by for his grandchildren and great-grandchildren.

Cesare's dog barked in the night, he heard the doctor come in downstairs, and the footsteps of his son and grandson. Then more footsteps: those of his son Matío, a soldier in the Alpine garrison stationed in town. He thought: Petar and Matío are here, but Cristiano, Engele, and Marco are in America. Giovanna should be here any minute.

The doctor came up the stairs and approached the bed; he had the lantern brought closer. He felt her pulse, then listened to her heart, placing his ear against her lean chest; he examined her eyes, bringing the light still closer; he made her sit up in bed and again thumped and listened to her chest and back. "You don't feel any pain?" he asked.

"I just feel cold and sort of weak," she replied.

"What did she say?" asked the doctor, who was young and didn't understand our language. And Tönle translated.

They went down to the kitchen and the doctor wrote a prescription. Petar went back to town with him so that he could then go to the pharmacist for the medicines.

She didn't want to take any medicine, only a little sheep's milk diluted with barley water (as was done to wean nursing babies).

Two days later she closed her eyes. Don Tita Müller came to administer the holy oil and after another three days she stopped breathing. Again the priest arrived with surplice and stole, and the bell ringer with the cross, and the horse caparisoned in black and yellow; the whole hamlet and the neighboring ones as well accompanied her to the hill behind the church, where for three centuries everyone had been laid to rest. When he got home, Tönle realized how empty the house was and the bed they had shared for all those years, even though for most months of the year he had had to be far away.

There were times when he thought he could see her poking the fire in the fireplace or sorting potatoes in the darkened room: he called out to her, but the figure vanished and he felt alone.

The harvest had been good that autumn: the potatoes healthy and abundant, a full weight of rye and barley, and the loft overflowed with sweet-smelling hay. Tönle took his sheep to graze on the lands leased by the community at the edge of the communal woods; in the early afternoon hours, on their return from school, he would be joined by a couple of grandchildren, Petar's children or Giovanna's, and together, after penning the animals in the Gluppa sheepfold, they went to the Hano copse to gather dry beech leaves, which they put in large rucksacks and carried home in the evening: these would serve as litter for the animals in winter and then as fertilizer in the spring.

It snowed in November, then the rain denuded the land, after which splendid sunshine made the meadows on the Spilleche bloom once more. Hoarfrost steamed on the cultivated soil during the warm hours of the day, and now with the war and all the emigrants who had returned, you saw many men at work on the slopes: after digging up the juniper and barberry bushes, they pickaxed the soil, putting the grassy turf and roots on one side, the black soil on the other and in a pile of stones, then with the larger stones they built a low dry wall, and in the empty space toward the mountain put the other stones, then the gravel and soil; on top of the soil they burned the stubble with the clods, roots, and bushes.

What was left from the combustion made excellent fertilizer. The land was thus ready for sowing and the harvest would be abundant for a couple of years—except that to prepare a few dozen square meters this way took weeks of work.

As always, ever since he had stopped having to go across the border, our Tönle worked that spring of 1915 at spreading manure on the cultivated plots. Carrying it, no—for now he was no longer able to shoulder the pannier; instead when he returned home in the evening, he carried on his back a bundle of dry branches for the fireplace, which was always eager for them. But his true passion was still to be with the sheep in the pastures; he knew them all, each and every one, by the color of their wool and their way of bleating even if they all seemed alike; he also knew each one's individual character: the one he had to keep an eye on because it had the habit of separating from the herd, the one that fed most voraciously on fresh grass wet with dew and was therefore apt to get a swollen belly, which lamb still tried to nurse at the mother even though it ought to have been weaned months ago, which one ruminated the longest. His old black dog then needed only a sign, not even a word, to understand his thought.

When one of his grandchildren came to join him in the afternoon, they had little to say to each other of an essential nature, but their words were so clear and natural and simple that the silences that followed were like meditations on the seasons, on work, on the woods, on the wild and domestic animals.

One day his grandson, returning from school, told him that Augusta the teacher had explained that Italy would soon go to war against Austria-Hungary to liberate Trent and

Trieste. She had even brought into the classroom the newspaper *Corriere della Sera,* in which it said that the great poet Gabriele d'Annunzio had made a speech on the very spot where Garibaldi had once departed for Sicily, and that everybody in the cities wanted war.

The spring of 1915 was an especially beautiful one in our parts. The March rains had melted the snow very quickly, and it really seemed that more than any other year in the past, the call of spring with the sound of bells and the bonfires on the Spilleche and the Moor, had awakened the vegetation in advance: no sooner had the snow trickled away in countless brooks than the meadows were all covered with white crocuses promptly visited by the bees, and by the middle of April the larches were filled with the chirping of grouse. By early May the beeches were bedecked in a beautiful shining green that stood out against the black of the firs. The cherry tree on the roof was like a necklace in the hair of a young girl, or a flowering cloud: the petals dropped from the still naked branches like light butterflies and fluttered on the thatch, which itself seemed to come back to life. Meanwhile, the cuckoo, which as always had announced its arrival on Saint Mark's Day, flew from one copse to another, repeating its cry: at times it sounded so close to people's houses it was as though it were trying to call someone. Due to the early rain and now an unusual heat, the grass in the meadows grew thick and fast.

Early on the morning of the twenty-fourth, Tönle had driven his sheep to the usual pastures; then he sat down to light his pipe and enjoy the day. First he heard something like a rumble in the sky, then a distant explosion. He stood up and looked around; he saw nothing but he still heard that rumble and explosion repeated, followed by others more numerous. Now he understood: the war had begun and the Campolongo and Verena forts were firing on those at Luserna and Vezzena.

Already at night he had thought he'd heard something of the kind, but perhaps the mountain range and the streams had carried most of the noise in another direction, so that yes, he had heard it, but so remote that he hadn't thought of cannon fire, but maybe dynamite explosions, far away, where they were working on the roads high up toward the Portule, trying to set up the big 280-caliber howitzers. And he'd gone back to sleep.

But they hadn't slept in town that night; the garrison and artillery commanders had already been put on the alert the morning of the twenty-third, and before dusk they knew of the declaration of war that Victor Emmanuel's ambassador had delivered to Franz Josef.

Lieutenant General Pasquale Oro, who was in command of the sector, issued a proclamation "to all the inhabitants" of our mountains. In resounding words he spoke of faith in victory, and of the liberation of our brothers beyond the frontier; then, more prosaically, he asked for the spontaneous cooperation of our fellow countrymen with the army. Such cooperation, when requested, was to be total and prompt. Otherwise it would be imposed.

That same night the reserves who had been recalled to military duty had left for the border, where the Ivrea and Treviso brigades were already massed. And no one in town went to bed that night, because they were all out on the road looking up toward the Trentino and toward our forts, waiting for the first bursts of fire from the batteries.

Around midnight they came. Half a minute after the burst

you heard the sound of the departing shot, and after a minute, far away and muffled by the mountains, that of the explosion. It had nothing to do with celebrations and fireworks this time, and no one had any wish to speak or make comments; children clutched their mothers' skirts, sweethearts clutched each other, and the old men smoked in silence. No, there could be no enthusiasm for those bursts of fire and those explosions: there they were, above their houses like a dark new threat, even more sinister than the sounds of the tocsin that announced a fire or heralded the armies that in previous centuries had descended into Italy from the north, bringing violence and death.

They waited on the road, our countryfolk, for the sun to rise and warm them a little; and later, as silently as they had gone out the past evening, they went back into their houses on that morning of 24 May 1915 and closed the door, although it was the custom in our little part of the world to keep one's door always open.

Thus it was that Tönle, that morning at daybreak, saw no smoke coming out of the chimneys, nor people moving around in their kitchen gardens or on the roads leading to the woods. At first he didn't pay much attention, but having heard those shots he understood the reason for it. For the third time, he mournfully relit his pipe; he felt sad and angry as well, almost to the point of feeling that he himself was a bad person because of the cruelty of governments and poets who wanted war. As for the generals, he thought, waging war is their profession, even if having people killed is the worst sort of profession; and maybe to be a soldier at the age of twenty, whether for this or that government or state, is like a game, an adventure, an opportunity to meet other people like yourself, as well as a chance to show your own strength, or even an appetite for rebellion like Tita Haus, whom Major von Fabini had had to send home as ungovernable after two years in the military stockade: on that occasion, he had had him flogged in front of the whole battalion drawn up in formation, and when it was over, he had got up from the trestle calm as could be, pulling up his pants. "Had enough, soldier?" said the major. "Don't forget, I have an iron will." And Tita Haus, having buttoned his pants, spat on the major's boots and replied, "You may have an iron will, but I've got a bronze ass." And so, since they had now tried everything, they sent him home.

All of which meant that one could be a soldier or not, but not shoot to kill among poor people. And besides, for whom? So thought Tönle, as he watched his sheep, smoked his pipe, and listened to the big guns on the other side of the valley.

FOUR

Almost every day, when it was time for the polenta, one heard at regular intervals that rumble of big guns, but life went on just the same: hay was dried in the meadows, potatoes were hoed, and firewood was collected in the woods in preparation for winter. When it was time to mow the meadows for the second time, there came an Italian infantry attack against the Austrian fortifications near the shepherds' huts at Vezzena; the divisions had emerged in formation from the pine woods with the band playing and the flag unfurled, the commanders in dress uniform and with their sabers unsheathed: this was how they expected to reach Trent. Instead there were many fatal casualties, with the wounded being taken to the new building that was supposed to serve as a hospital for our population.

That summer, for the first time since 1866, there was no smuggling between our mountains and the Valsugana, nor did emigrants take the high road now that the Tyrolese, who had once given them hospitality when they stopped along the way, were mobilized into battalions of *Standschutzen* to defend the borders. It was thus impossible to go from one country to the other because the soldiers and patrols fired, and they certainly weren't like the revenue and customs agents from whom one had been able to buy one's transit for a lira; now you could only die for nothing at all.

Even to pasture your flocks near the borders was forbidden, and for the first time in centuries a dozen Alpine huts were left deserted. The inhabitants who had not been called up for the war, namely men over fifty and boys between fourteen and nineteen, were mobilized to dig trenches and build roads; and along the carriage tracks that snaked up the sides of the mountains and were not exposed to the eyes of the enemy, the big 149-caliber cannons were dragged by hand and then installed in batteries in positions poorly defended by fir trunks, larchwood planks, and sacks of earth.

Two of Tönle's sons, Matío and Petar, along with their comrades from the hamlet, the neighboring hamlets, and the town, were at the front lines with the Alpine battalion between Porta Renzola and the Mandriolo; the other three sons, who were in America, had written a letter in which they said they wouldn't come home to get shot, but only if they were offered good jobs. And if these were not their exact words, this was surely the meaning. Thus, now with two sons going to war at the front, three working in America, his daughters married, his wife dead, and the years beginning to take their toll on his legs, our Bintarn had to work harder; to be sure, his daughters-in-law and even the children helped and took care of the kitchen garden, the potato and lentil plots, the barley, and the hens, while all that was left for him was to see to the flock and to firewood for the winter, and though there weren't that many sheep, now that the high pastures were forbidden and grazing was permitted in the woods along the paths and in the clearings, it was harder to control them because sometimes they went into the underbrush to lie down and chew their cud in peace, which made it difficult to round them up to go home. And when he made a trip to collect firewood, he arrived at the end of the path with a load of it on his back and his legs weary.

But if the war thus caused no few inconveniences among our shepherds, herdsmen, charcoal burners, smugglers, and woodcutters, to others in the provincial seat it meant profits. All the hotels were occupied by officials and journalists, the restaurants by army messes; and innkeepers, delicatessen owners, tradesmen, bakers, laundresses, and streetwalkers, in short, all those of either sex who had dealings with the army or its followers, did very well.

On the level ground at the hamlet of Schbanz they had built large hangars that could have housed more than a hundred sheep, but instead they put airplanes in them that had landed from the sky. One day Tönle's grandson, on his return from school, went straight to the Hano woods to tell his grandfather that the poet Gabriele d'Annunzio, now a commander, as the school principal Müller had explained, had flown with these airplanes all the way to the sky over the city of Trent, and there had dropped leaflets and the Italian flag. Tönle, on hearing this story, shook his head and drew sharply on his pipe. The first time he had seen those big birds flying noisily over the Valle d'Assa, his astonishment had been mingled with scorn: they were nothing but diabolical contraptions for making war and who could say how many lire they cost, and how much flour for polenta one could have bought to feed people, or how many sheep. And if for them there were borders, what good were they if they could fly over them with airplanes? And if there were no borders in the air, why should there be any on land? And by this "for them" he meant all those who held the borders to be something concrete or sacred; while for him and those like him—who weren't as few as they might seem, but the majority of men—borders had never existed except as guards to be paid off or gendarmes to avoid. In short, if the air was free and the water was free, the land also ought to be free.

Early in that first winter of war, his sons who had been stationed on those borders came home on leave. They were thus able to bring with them on a sled a good supply of wood, which he had stored at the foot of the Gluppa.

After these leaves of absence, the battalion was transferred to the Alta Carnia front, because those who were running the war said it was more needed there. But actually it was rumored that our Alpine troops had been moved because this front was too quiet, and besides, being so close to their families they hadn't shown the proper aggressive spirit in the face of the enemy.

That year the snow came fairly early to cover our mountains, and by November the dark woods of the Dhor were already tinged with white; in the haylofts under the wide, steep roofs of the houses hay and dry leaves were stored for the winter and in the cellars below there were potatoes, cabbages, and barley.

If it hadn't been for the regular shellings toward noon aimed by the Italian batteries at the Austrian fortifications, one might almost have believed that this first winter of war was just the same as many other past winters. But certainly not in town, where there was a continuous movement of soldiers, trucks, horses, carabinieri; the rack railway went puffing up the mountain carrying munitions and weapons and news from various fronts of the war, which already was being called a world war as though that were progress. One day the king of Italy even came, Victor Emmanuel III, dressed as an ordinary soldier.

At Christmas they sang the old and traditional carols, but only the people of the hamlets performed them in our old language, thereby arousing protests by the military authorities since they thought the words might be anti-Italian. So for the Christmas rites in church, except for *Adeste fideles,* people sang insipid little songs.

The days passed as though muffled by snow, and during the evening vigils in the stables there was no talk of Odin or Loki or of the Guardian Spirits that the Council of Trent had relegated once and for all to the Val di Nos, or of work in faraway lands, but only of the war, which had taken away men who were fit to work on the roads of the world. And if someone died while working on the roads of the world, it wasn't like on the battlefield: you worked for your own needs and your family's, while now on the battlefields you died for nothing. Therefore, when death notices arrived, brought by the carabinieri or the municipal courier, grief was accompanied by a feeling of bitter rage.

In Nappa's stable, they leafed slowly by the light of the lamp through *The Italian War: Illustrated Chronicle History of Events,* a weekly periodical published by the Casa Sonzogno in Milan, and which cost twenty centesimi. But there were some news items and illustrations that—here where the war, you might say, was at people's doors—aroused confusion and doubt, even though for simple minds printed words and pictures sometimes have the force of absolute truth.

One cover showed a soldier decked out in a kind of armor, with helmet, kneepieces, and lance, like a crusader, or a Greek in the Trojan War as depicted in a Remondini print. A news item, on the other hand, reported that our troops, occupying an Alpine shelter, "found written in Italian on two stones in the wall, to which a hook was attached, the inscription THERE IS MONEY HERE—PULL! Instead the opening contained a loaded bomb!" And in another item: "The swarms of arrows hurled from above by airplanes are terrible weapons that in falling attain a dreadful force of penetration." These things, thus described, and the reproduction of photographs of gigantic cannons, or one of a path where our emigrants had once descended into the Valsugana, with the caption, "The Austrian barricade in the Trentino with electrified fences," provoked remarks, including ironical ones, and discussions that some high commanders would have called defeatist.

In the last days of February the children summoned the spring as in every other past year, by ringing cow bells and running barefoot on the still snowy meadows; but the military authorities had sternly forbidden the lighting of bonfires on the hilltops since they could be taken as signals to the enemy. And maybe because the bonfires weren't lit, the month of March brought, instead of sun and rain, more snow and day after day of cold wind.

But meanwhile people were saying that the imperial troops must be getting ready for an offensive; it appeared that some Czech deserters and a soldier from Trent crossing to this side of the line had reported that they were setting up batteries of hundreds of cannons, big ones that fired shells weighing ten quintals; that a number of regiments had been withdrawn from the Balkans and the Russian front and were moving south from the Tyrol, and that the archduke Eugene in person and the crown prince Karl would direct the invasion of our lands. But it was also said that our military commands didn't want to believe all this.

Just as the tail end of winter was cold and harsh, the spring was sudden and mild: as the days suddenly got longer, so did the snow quickly melt, and the cuckoo's song made the woods bloom. In the hamlets, women working in the kitchen gardens raised their heads to listen with sadness and desire for their men far away in the war. Tönle Bintarn, however, his pipe ever clenched between his teeth, became daily more silent and morose: he left the house at dawn and didn't return until evening; and in leaving and approaching the old house he always raised his eyes to the cherry tree on the roof to see if the buds were swelling and the flowers blossoming.

One May evening on the Moor, while he was gazing with unusual persistence at the sheep and the landscape, he heard the long, slow tolling of the passing bell. The peals, pulsing and regularly spaced, spread insistently over the meadows and woody hilltops, drowning out the singing of birds and the now habitual distant rumble of cannons toward the borders. His heart felt tormented by our pleasant landscape and that long, lonely sound of a bell, and he wondered which of his fellow countrymen could have died.

He lit his pipe, and that evening he himself came to think of death, not with anxiety and fear, but as repose, a state of resting forever in a landscape to be gazed at like this one. This is how it had surely been for his wife when in that autumn one of their sons carried her down on his back from the potato field.

When, after he had penned the sheep and given the dog a slice of polenta, he came down from the mountain and arrived home, his daughter-in-law told him she'd heard that the lawyer Bischofar had died. She had had the news from a woman who had been to town to sell eggs.

Sitting next to the fireplace, he ate two slices of polenta

and a piece of bacon fat along with a bowl of greens, then lit his pipe and watched the dying embers. He remembered the old lawyer, who had always called him friend—or rather *main ksèl*—and when they met, maybe two or three times a year, always spoke to him in the old tongue and even knew the specific terms used by shepherds. But Tönle did not forget the good he had done for the family when he had had to flee from his homeland over that business with the king's revenue agents, and so at Christmas he had always taken him half a lamb, for which the lawyer would by all means try to pay him or exchange something. He smoked his pipe and watched the fire as it was going out, and meanwhile twilight was entering the smoky kitchen and blurring the outlines of objects. Tomorrow, he thought, I'll go down and pay him my respects.

The next morning he shaved carefully and washed himself, from the wardrobe took the wool and cotton suit that he wore only for solemn occasions, cleaned and greased his shoes, and, his pipe clenched between his now blackened teeth, went down into town.

The old man in his nineties lay there in a coffin in his office; the pictures on the walls of famous or illustrious persons with a friendly dedication had been shrouded, making the bookshelves seem to come closer to the visitors. Flowers, so many flowers: roses, narcissus, clusters of cytisus, cornflowers, geraniums in bunches and in large vases occupied the whole space near the windows, and their aroma masked the odor of the candles. Many people were going up and down the stairs of the old house, which stood opposite the unique, fifteenth-century Palazzo dei Sette, or rather *Siben alten Kameun prudere libe.*

Bintarn, too, went up the stairs and entered the office. He

paid no attention to the white-haired priest seated in a corner, the family members and relatives of the grand old man in the coffin, the authorities, or the townsfolk. He stood there motionless for a while in front of the coffin, as though he had taken root in the white planking of the floor, which made those who were crowding behind him grumble and push. Everyone was astonished and looked frightened when he finally said in a loud voice, "*Palle odar spete de leute allesamont sterben!*"—Everybody dies sooner or later.

"Amen!" responded the old priest with equal vigor from the corner where he was sitting.

Tönle bowed slightly to the coffin where his old friend lay, put his hat on his head, and left, brushing past people in order to hurry back to the Moor.

Three days later it was 15 May and the cherry tree on the roof opened its blossoms. The petals, like snowflakes on windless mountain pastures, settled on the thatch that covered the house.

Tönle went out early. In the doorway he refilled his pipe and lit it, looked at the tree, the meadows down the slope where the grass was growing in abundance, and set out to get his sheep. He opened the fence, urged the dog to drive them up toward the Petareitle pasture, and followed along, at a steady pace timed by his stick, letting them graze here and there along the edge of the road bounded by stone markers on the side of the meadows and arable land.

Once he had arrived up there, he sat down under a fir tree and took from his pocket a couple of potatoes he had roasted the night before under the ashes in the fireplace. The dog sat beside him, awaiting his portion of crisp, tasty skins.

Suddenly he thought he heard from the direction of the border the sound of an airplane, or "pigeon," as it was called; then he saw it emerge high in the sky above our town, immediately followed by two others, thus forming a triangle. He did not pay much attention, but once again he thought of all the labor and capital that was being wasted by the war.

Visits by these "Rumpler C1 pigeons" were not unusual. They came from far away, perhaps from Trent or Mattarello, flew over and went away after the sentinel on the bell tower had sounded the alarm and the soldiers had fired a few useless volleys. This time, however, they persisted in their flight, circling again and again like buzzards over a brood hen until Eugenio sounded the big bell, the one that in hot months made the dark, leaden clouds dissolve into hail. He was ringing the tocsin as he did for fire, which too often burned our houses with their roofs of shingles or thatch. The tolling radiated in the morning air and now was the only sound heard, not the birds singing or the airplanes. The voice of the big bell had silenced all other voices.

Tönle got to his feet, leaning with both hands on his stick; then he heard something like the dull, dark buzz of a huge insect come out of the sky from over the mountains, then absolute silence, and down below, toward the Hort, a flash and a great cloud of rising smoke, and afterward a roar to make the mountains tremble to their roots. He stood there in dismay.

It was "Long George," the 350-mm cannon that fired shells weighing 750 kilos for thirty kilometers; it had given the signal for the "punitive expedition."

The roar had not yet spent itself among the hills and valleys when at regular intervals more such shells fell on the town; announced from afar by a deep hum, they exploded among the houses, shattering walls and roofs, burning, and killing.

Since he was far away and high up, he certainly could not hear the fearful cries of the women and children, the yelling of the soldiers, the orders of the commanders, but he could well imagine what was happening in town. He had also noticed that to the regular roar of the explosions, and the sound of the airplanes still circling above like buzzards, had now been added a distant and continuous rumble, like intense, uninterrupted shelling. And this was because the Austrian infantry offensive had begun near the Vezzene.

Tönle received all these unhappy signals and imagined the people and town under the fire of the huge cannon, and felt within himself a raging rebellion against everything and everybody; smoking and cursing, he drove the sheep into the depths of the woods, in order not to see or hear anything more. But he was unable to hold out for long. He drove the sheep out again, siccing the dog on them, penned them in the sheepfold, and went down to his house.

It was perhaps a little past noon, many columns of smoke rose from the town, and the pungent odor from the fires and explosions irritated even the throats of tobacco smokers. As he entered the kitchen, he saw his grandchildren who had run home from school, still in a state of excitement over the unforeseeable interruption. They were telling their mother confused and frightening things, and she, who meanwhile had spilled the polenta on the chopping board, was walking senselessly back and forth looking for the knife she was holding in her hand.

Tönle reproached himself for the rage and vexation he had felt before in the woods, and in a steady voice tried to restore calm, making them all sit down quietly and eat. But it was worse in the silence because the explosions of the big shells and the distant rumble did more to increase the anxiety and fear than the children's confused words and their mother's agitation. But, on the other hand, the old man felt certain that the shelling could not reach the hamlet, for the Moor acted as a shield and all the houses lay in a dead angle.

In the early hours of the afternoon a detachment of carabinieri reached the hamlet, but this time there were no smugglers to arrest. Loudly they called all the people out into the road, some twenty persons, to say that by order of the military authorities in accord with the civil ones, all the inhabitants were to evacuate their houses and go down to the plain, where they would find lodging and assistance. And all this as soon as possible, because the danger was great. They were to leave their doors and windows open, and take with them only the most necessary things. Perhaps in a few days they would be able to come back. Having said this, the carabinieri went away to shout the order in the other hamlets.

That evening the fires lighted up the sky, and Tönle accompanied his daughter-in-law and grandchildren to his daughter Giovanna's house at Prudeghar. In the handcart that they used for firewood he had put a few household items and a sack with clothes and blankets; around his daughter-in-law's neck he had tied a little leather bag containing a hundred lire in silver pieces. There at Prudeghar, families were reunited in groups, and women, old men, children, and babies would leave before dawn by back roads, avoiding the bombarded town; once they had reached the Luka woods, they would descend into the plain by the Camporossignolo road. Tönle brusquely said good-bye to his daughter, daughter-in-law, and grandchildren, grumbled something to the effect that he was going home, and if things got worse he would join them later, with the sheep.

Although by now he had seen and endured many things and happenings in the world, never had he seen people's houses like this, so empty, silent, and wretched. Like an abandoned beehive, or a plundered nest. And amid all those doors and shutters left wide open to the war, he shut himself up in his own house as he had never done before, not even when he was wanted by the police. He retired to the bedroom, using an ashwood pole to bar even that door, which he had always kept half-open.

He didn't sleep, and in the great silence of his house, where one had been able to hear the voices of the beams, and of the hamlet that spoke with the creaking of its windows (oh, how he would have liked to hear the rain on the roof and the breeze among the branches of the cherry tree!), the sounds of distant and nearby shelling and the crackle of fires continued to be shattering.

It was still dark when he got up, and opening the window to the south, the one facing the town, he tied his shoes by the glow of the distant flames. Then he went out and climbed the mountain.

These were not like the holiday fireworks of the night of 1 January 1900 when, unable to participate with the rest of his fellow countrymen, he had lit his bonfire in front of the cross on Mount Katz: then there had been joy and brass bands, now fear and weeping, and though involved in both occasions, this one now and the other in the past, he could only participate in solitude.

From up there he saw the dawn, and then people moving along the roads that led from the hamlets to the plain, and divisions of soldiers coming up from the plain on foot or on bicycles and meeting our refugees. Meanwhile, in all this, the sounds of battle kept getting louder.

He filled his pipe, lit it, looked at the time, and turned to his sheep, driving them once more into the deepest part of the woods.

That day squads of soldiers, carabinieri, and revenue agents passed through inhabited centers and isolated houses to make sure that the mass exodus was total. But they still found a few laggards, who through indifference to the danger or rude obstinacy, defied fires and bombs and the orders of generals in the hope of saving something they needed more: money, or clothing and linen, or simply memories. The smoke over the houses was oppressive, and neither the geraniums in the windows, the orchards, or the meadows in bloom succeeded in mitigating the ugliness and repulsion of that blackish yellow smoke; just as the singing of larks and finches in the more remote and quieter corners could not make itself heard amid the voices of despair.

In the afternoon Tönle emerged in a clearing and saw that down in the town even the bell tower was on fire. Perhaps an incendiary bomb had struck the belfry, igniting the wooden trusses that supported the bells. Raging and heartbroken, he cried out: "*Alle inzòart!*"—That's the end! And he began beating at a bush with his stick. When he had calmed down, he looked once again at the bell tower, recalling that many years ago his mother and grandmother had been among the women who had donated their gold earrings to be melted down in the bronze of the bells to make the sound more harmonious.

More days went by. There were no civilians left in the houses, and even the soldiers being hastily sent to the front to stem the offensive sought to avoid inhabited places and were made to march at night. Tönle spent the whole day in the woods with his sheep and dog, and when evening came and he could no longer make out the cherry tree on the roof, he emerged, wary as a fox, from the edge of the woods and went into his house to rest for a couple of hours and eat something.

One thing that bothered him was that he couldn't light a fire. In these miserable, abandoned places food was now more plentiful than it had been for ages, for inside the wide-open houses you could find potatoes, bacon fat, pieces of cheese, barley and lentils, even some pieces of smoked meat; emaciated hens and rabbits wandered through the yards and empty stables, almost as though seeking the company of the owners, and now it wasn't hard for some stray soldier to catch a few.

One evening Tönle went into the house of the Pûne family, which had once been full of boys and girls and now stood silent and wide open. A swarm of bees that no one had collected had settled on the plum tree in front of the house, and stray cats reigned in the doorway. He went in the kitchen, saying in a loud voice, "May I?" as he used to do when the inhabitants of the house were there.

He entered the silence, and stood a while in the doorway looking at the shelves above the copper pans, where he knew they kept the bottle of spirits with gentian. The bottle was still there in its usual place, along with the two shot glasses placed upside down to keep them from being dirtied by flies. He took the dark glass bottle and a glass, sat down on the straw chair next to the hearth, poured himself a shot full to the brim, and drank, looking at the spent ashes. When he got up to put the bottle and glass back where they belonged, the darkness of evening had already entered the house; he closed the door again, and gazed down at the fire and smoke still rising over the town.

The next morning, at dawn, he decided to visit the Nappas' stable. The chains hung idly from the manger, where there was still hay that the cows hadn't had time to eat; the litter was strewn all over with dung. So he took the crabgrass broom from behind the door and swept the passageway. He even collected the women's spindles and reels, which had been abandoned there, and carried them into the room between the stable and the kitchen, where a hemp and linen fabric was in progress on the loom. He was overcome by nostalgia for those evenings when they would all get together to tell their stories and sometimes sing the song of the *eisenponnar.*

In the last ten days of May the sun turned unusually hot for this season, causing the meadows to be choked with grass that grew visibly taller from one day to the next; on the terraces where they had been sown, barley and rye, potatoes and flax, oats and lentils thrived better than in any other past year, as though all this were nature's revenge on the war of men. Tönle would have been able to pasture his little flock at night in this deserted abundance, but the idea never even occurred to him. Nor did he want to give up his home and go with his sheep and dog down to the plain, where relatives and neighbors had already been for days; he felt as though he were the custodian of the belongings they had all left behind, and his presence was like a sign, a symbol, of peaceful life against the violence of the war. He thought also of his old lawyer friend, to whom he had said good-bye for the last time ten days before, and of his wife, who had been carried down from the potato field on Saint Matthew's Day and now lay in the cemetery behind the church. But the church had been almost destroyed, the bell tower demolished by shells and its bells smashed, and the graves in the cemetery devastated by bombs.

From his lookout places in the woods he observed the soldiers as they passed, in battalions and regiments, on their way to the battle. One day the shelling became very heavy. Then it stopped.

The silence was more frightening than the rumble of battle, and that day crows and ravens were emboldened to take possession of the yards, kitchen gardens, and our abandoned houses. Tönle saw groups of soldiers in disorder, without commanders, some disarmed and even wounded, making their way from the Dhor down toward Prudeghar; still others marched in ranks up through the woods, and in silence took the paths for the higher mountains.

The next day the fighting resumed closer, the cannons started firing from this side of the Assa valley, setting fire to more houses and scattered villages. Toward evening—but there were no more bells to sound the hour of vespers—a dark thunderstorm grew thick over the Wassa-Gruba, and with flashes of lightning, roars of thunder, and hail, burst in the direction of the Mosciagh. Simultaneously with the storm, the Austrians unleashed an attack on the same mountain with salvos of cannons, bursts of machine-gun fire, hand grenades, mortars, and rifles, so that the one roar and the other, in the sky and on earth, blended into a hellish fury.

Tönle, having taken shelter at the edge of the Gharto woods under a fir tree whose branches drooped to the ground, listened with trepidation to this Dies Irae, and through the branches of the fir tree saw the flashes from sky and mountain. It was as though he were enchained by that spectacle of disaster, unable to take his eyes from it or move his feet to go away.

Once nature and man had subsided, he again heard the water dripping from the branches, but also, in the distance, he made out the cries of wounded men, and, finally, a single, isolated burst of gunfire in the Sichestal woods.

That same night, when he went back down to his house, he decided to take as much food and tobacco as he could carry. But in the hamlet he ran into a disorderly group of soldiers who were looting; enraged and clenching his stick as though it were a rifle, he began yelling in German, and they ran away in surprise, thinking perhaps that the enemy was arriving. Instead of remaining in his house, he went to spend the night in the shelter under the cliff where he had hidden fifty years before after hitting the king's revenue agent. He had left his sheep, guarded by the dog, among the Kheldar rocks, where it would be very hard for anyone not used to the place to find them.

The next day calm seemed to have returned; the surviving soldiers from the divisions that had gone up through the woods toward the mountains to the north turned back, retraced their steps through the meadows and valley, and retreating south of the town, which was still burning, began digging defenses in the woods and on the heights that blocked access to the plain.

At dawn Tönle ate a piece of smoked meat, lit his pipe, and in the new silence returned to his sheep. The dog wagged its tail in welcome and the sheep bleated. He descended with his little flock into open country and led it to graze on community land, where for too many days the grass had not been cropped and had grown as never before.

In the afternoon he saw a suspicious patrol emerge from

the woods, and from its behavior and uniforms realized they were Austrians. Moving cautiously and crouching behind the stone markers at the edge of the roads, they advanced all the way to the town, which by now was completely destroyed. It was the twenty-eighth of May.

Just as before he had avoided the soldiers of the Royal Italian Army, so now, even more cautiously, he tried to avoid the soldiers of the Imperial and Royal Austro-Hungarian Army. The fighting, however, had shifted south of our town, where fierce resistance was being mounted, and for whole days and whole nights those wooded hilltops were continually rent by cannon and mortar fire, and the woods ripped by machine guns.

Tönle watched and listened, staying always hidden in the depths of the woods, cocking an ear at every passing sound so as not to be surprised or robbed of his sheep. Afternoons, as he huddled in some gorge like a wild animal, thoughts would sometimes come to him of his dead wife, his lawyer friend, or of the time when he worked as a gardener at the castle in Prague. Oddly enough, he didn't think about his three sons who had emigrated to America, or the two who were fighting in the Alpine troops, or his grandchildren, his daughters, or his daughters-in-law who had fled to the plain on the second day of the bombardment.

One evening—it was the ninth of June—he decided to go back and sleep in his house. Leaving his sheep with the dog at the Kheldar rocks, he went down at a rapid and determined pace toward the abandoned hamlet.

The flares from the combat, to which he'd become accustomed, first lighted up the path for him and then the house. As he entered, he realized at once that soldiers had been there too, but perhaps because of the poverty of the house itself and its furnishings they had done no serious damage; all the same they had left their mark, dirtying the kitchen, overturning all the drawers, and burning a chair in the fireplace. But the two old prints, the one of the bear hunt and the one of wolves attacking a sleigh, were still where his son Petar had hung them when he was just a boy, that first year on the run. He brought over a chair and took them down from the wall, and the whiteness of the plaster underneath was like a blank space on the smoke-blackened walls. He looked around for a place to hide them, and finally decided to stick them under a beam in the stable.

On his way back to the kitchen, he stepped on human excrement in the doorway; he was instantly enraged and, cursing, took the crabgrass broom and threw the filth outside. He took a bucket of rainwater from the cistern and sloshed it over the stone floor, swept out the water, put everything back in order, and finally closed the door and retired to his bedroom, the one he had always dreamed of while wandering through the world and had enjoyed for so many winters.

From his vest pocket he took out his watch to rewind it, then meaning to hook it by its ring from the usual nail near the headboard of the bed. But before hanging it, he held it in his hand to feel its weight and hear its ticking, and even though in the gloom he wasn't able to see what time it was, he saw the movement of the hammer pounded by the quarryman to the tempo of the seconds, and by the touch of his fingers felt the words embossed around the dial, and on the back, also embossed, the representation of a mine shaft, with posts, a lantern, and two miners. He had bought this watch many years ago on his way through Ulm, and it was engraved with the slogans of the socialist workers who were just then beginning their struggle for the reduction of working hours. The embossed inscriptions said in German: "We want eight hours to work—Eight hours to learn—Eight hours to rest." And again: "For social harmony, brotherhood, and unity." Weighing the watch in the palm of his hand, he thought: They used to work for sixteen or more hours in the mines, and now instead of brotherhood there's the war, and the poor are killing each other . . .

He hung the watch on the nail, took off his shoes, stretched out on the bed, and pulled an old blanket over himself. From a distance there still came that glow of fires and the flashes of cannons, and the continuous noise, sometimes louder, sometimes subdued.

Toward morning he heard footsteps approaching the house and violent knocking at the door. He did not move from the bed, and thought: Ah, if I'd left the door open, no one would have knocked; a closed door when all the other ones are open means there's someone inside, and that's something soldiers know. They pounded harder, breaking the latch, and the door banged against the wall. He heard someone walking through the kitchen and going in the stable, and again he thought: Let's hope he doesn't find my tobacco. The soldier came back in the kitchen and climbed the stairs.

The bedroom door was also flung open, and squinting his eyes in the half-darkness he saw a boy in uniform pause for a moment on the threshold to look around and then rest his gaze on the bed where Tönle was pretending to be asleep. Attracted by the ticking and glitter of the watch hanging over the headboard, he approached slowly and reached out his hand to take it. Tönle opened his eyes and growled in German, "Don't touch it, stupid!"

The soldier froze, and when he came to himself, he ran from the room, stumbling down the stairs. Tönle also got up as soon as the soldier got out to the yard; he quickly put on his shoes and went down to the stable to retrieve his pipe tobacco, which, twisted into a cord, he had hidden under the straw in the farthest corner. But as he emerged, he found at the door of the house an Austrian patrol commanded by a second lieutenant, who came up to him immediately, saying in Italian, "You're a spy and you're under arrest!"

Tönle spat his saliva, dark with tobacco, on the ground, muttering something that the officer didn't completely understand and therefore asked, still in Italian, "What are you talking about? Come along!"

"I've got to take the sheep to the pasture," the old man replied in German, "and I don't have time to waste with soldiers." He started to walk away, but at a sign from the lieutenant, two soldiers blocked his path and took him by the arms. He wrenched himself free, but no longer having the agility he had once had, he was immediately seized again and held fast.

"You old devil!" said the lieutenant in German, with a Viennese accent. "Now we'll fix you. We're taking you to headquarters to hear what you have to say. We'll have you shot!"

"Mister officer," said the old man, aping the Viennese accent, which made the soldiers start laughing, "you're just a boy who doesn't understand a thing. I'm telling you I've got to take the sheep to the pasture."

They put him between them and made him walk in the

direction of the Pûne family's house; crouching over as they walked through the hamlet of Grabo, they reached Petareitle, where in 1909 Matío Parlío had built his house isolated from the world; it was here that the Austrians had now set up their regimental headquarters. Field kitchens were being laid out behind the house, and soldiers were coming and going: some were digging, others carrying wood, still others water from the Prunnele stream; in Nicola Scoa's sheepfold they had apparently set up a medical station, for there were other soldiers with conspicuous bandages resting nearby.

Many curious soldiers gathered at once around the old man, whispering among themselves; a corporal came over and handed him a cup of hot coffee, and he took it without saying a word. After drinking it slowly under the eyes of all the soldiers clustered around him, he handed back the empty cup, saying, "Thanks, corporal."

"You speak German, grandpa?" the corporal asked him.

"Yes," he replied, "before you ever did." And he refused to say another word.

Then they escorted him into the house, to the kitchen, where a major, leaning with his hands on the edge of the table, was studying topographical maps that were spread out on it. The second lieutenant who had brought him stood respectfully two paces away, and certainly he had already explained the situation.

"So," the major said suddenly, standing upright, "you have sheep to take to pasture. And where are they?"

"At the Kheldar rocks."

"And how many are there?"

"Twenty-seven with the lambs." But the old man said lambs in our dialect, and the major didn't understand.

"With what?"

"With the virgin sheep," he replied. At which the lieutenant smiled, putting a hand in front of his mouth.

"Why didn't you leave with the others when we started bombarding?"

"Why. Because my house is here and I'm an old man."

"Did you first meet or speak with any Italian officers?"

"With nobody!"

"And where did the sharpshooters go who were on Mount Mosciagh?"

"I don't know."

"Why do you speak German so well?"

"Why, always why. I was a soldier in Bohemia, and later I worked in all the lands ruled by the emperor Franz Josef."

"Who was your commander in Bohemia?"

"Major Fabini."

"Field Marshal von Fabini, maybe that's who you mean. But then you're a faithful subject," said the major with a certain enthusiasm.

"No," he replied. "I'm just a little shepherd and an old proletarian socialist."

"Then you're a spy for the Italians and that's why you stayed behind!"

"To hell with you and the Italians. Let me go about my business."

But the major also lost patience and signaled to the two escorting soldiers, who took him outside behind the house.

Half an hour later the second lieutenant came with a corporal. They took him with them and followed him along the path on the Platabech to the Kheldar rocks to find out if the story of the sheep was true. And two hours later they brought him back with the sheep and the black dog.

F I V E

Grazing sheep under armed escort had never been his experience, nor had he ever heard of such a thing, and the two Styrian soldiers assigned to this task almost enjoyed themselves like city boys as they followed him with his flock through hidden places out of range of the Italian artillery; but after three days, still along paths protected from the big guns—and he knew these paths better than the military men who studied them on topographical maps—they set about crossing the old borders. Day and night the cannons south of the valley discharged their loads on the lines of communication, or on presumed Austro-Hungarian rallying points or command centers or storage dumps. Tönle slowly took the longest route, and the two soldiers were glad to go along.

They passed through places where the battle had raged at the end of May, and the signs of it were still evident: cannons blown up and abandoned, baggage wagons, matériel of all kinds, the charred remains of fires, dried-up woods, and pastures ripped by bombs. Also the corpses of animals and men.

He did not care to look at all these things and these results, but they were there whether he looked or not, and he felt their effect like a shadow, with the sheep and the escort of two soldiers. In the Sichestal woods, they went quickly past thirteen Italian soldiers lying dead one next to another, with no insignia, badges, or chevrons, and one of the escort told him that they must have been shot by their own comrades in accordance with some order from on high. Not far from this place, a few soldiers who spoke Croatian among themselves were digging a ditch, and their rifles were stacked under a fir tree.

Our old man remembered the evening—it was the twenty-eighth or twenty-ninth of May—when after the storm and battle he had heard the sound of a fusillade.

They proceeded by the Dhorbellele, where they had once made him take his sheep during target practice; on Mount Kuko, among the mountain pines and rhododendrons, he again saw soldiers lying as though asleep, and again one of the escort explained that they were Italian soldiers killed in the battle of 26 May; and that he himself had been there, on the Portule peak.

They descended into the Valle d'Assa; divisions of Austrians who were resting at the springs, stretched out under the fir trees, gazed with curiosity at the old man with his sheep and escort, and quipped ironically among themselves about these odd prisoners.

Finally they reached the road, that same road he had taken so many times to go to work across the border, and the cannon fire and sounds of battle, which had never let up so that even the sheep had got used to them, were left behind.

At Vezzena they met a group of officers with field glasses and kit bags, on their way to Italy with a contingent of troops, who in passing stopped to look at this strange company, and young Lieutenant Fritz Lang came over to speak with one of the soldiers of the escort and with the old man. Tönle, who had decided not to talk to anyone anymore, made no reply to the officer's questions. He did not even answer when he actually saw, at the center of the group, his old commander from Budejovice, Major von Fabini, being paid every formal sign of respect by those around him.

Field Marshal von Fabini, now commander of the Eighth Mountain Division of the Twentieth Army Corps under the archduke Karl, margrave of Asiago, stared for a moment at that dirty, ragged old man. For a moment it also seemed to him that he was again seeing or recognizing something; finally he detached his left hand from his belt, made a vague gesture, and proceeded on his way toward the Val d'Astico, followed by his staff. The others, too, went on their way: Tönle and his sheep, I mean, with the black dog and the armed escort.

They stopped for the night between Santa Giuliana and Centa, where the steep slope of the Menador ended. The next day they went down to Pergine, and here without offering any explanation he entered a peasant house where, every spring, our emigrants would always stop to refresh themselves before resuming the road to Ulm. But the house was empty and abandoned; the disorder and the straw on the floor showed that the last inhabitants had been soldiers in transit.

At Pergine the gendarmes came and took charge of him. Reluctantly the two soldiers of the escort started back for the front after bidding him effusive good-byes. The gendarmes penned the sheep and dog in an abandoned stable and put him on the train for Trent.

All his protests had been useless, as useless as the barking of the dog and the bleating of the sheep. Still under escort, he arrived at the police station, where two days later they again interrogated him.

It was during the interrogation that his loud, angry voice was heard by his dog and sheep, which, as though in transhumance, were being taken by soldiers through the street and were passing under the windows. Hearing the sheep baaing and the dog barking, he rushed to the window, to the surprise of the gendarmes and the officer who was interrogating him, and began yelling in shepherd fashion, whereupon the whole flock stopped, blocking the street and the passage of an artillery division.

There was no way to budge the sheep and dog, and in the end they had to let him go out in the street and take his place at the head of the flock, to be escorted like a king across the city, to the astonishment of the few civilians and the too many soldiers.

They proceeded like this as far as Gardolo, but there they separated him for good from his animals, issuing him a stamped receipt. They put him on a troop train for the Brenner, and took him to an internment camp at Katzenau, where there were already other civilians.

These were the saddest days of his life. The rage and scorn he had felt during the days of his arrest gave way in his mind to a gloomy depression that made him forbidding and disliked by the other internees, civilians from Rovereto and the Valsugana.

The near total lack of tobacco made it impossible for him to observe the rules imposed by von Richer, the camp commandant. He ate little because whenever he had the opportunity, he traded his slice of black, poorly baked bread for a pinch of pipe tobacco, and the evening soup he gave secretly to a little girl who reminded him too much of one of his granddaughters. He was even tempted to barter his watch for tobacco, but one evening, after holding it in the palm of his hand for a whole hour, he decided no: too many things in life were connected with those hours, those movements of wheels and springs, and the inscriptions around the dial. It would be like renouncing everything he had ever been. Whereupon he clenched his blackened teeth on the stem of his pipe and almost broke it.

Time, in this forced idleness, passed very slowly and seemed besides to weigh on his spirit tenfold. In just a few months his hair had become completely white, and the lines in his face were as sunken as fissures on an eroded mountain; even his hands had become bony and had lost their strength.

One day, under escort and with two fellow prisoners, he was sent to help the peasants harvest potatoes in the fields; it was as though he had been reborn, but only for that day, because when they brought him back inside the barracks and barbed-wire fences, his mood was even more glum, although he had managed to smuggle a few kilos of potatoes into the camp. He gave some to the mother of the little girl, who called him grandfather, and the rest he traded for tobacco.

That same evening, at sundown, he sought out a quiet corner where he could smoke his pipe and give himself over to memories and nostalgia. But a guard, who perhaps shared his state of mind, came over to talk.

"Good evening, grandpa," he said. "How goes it?"

"I'm smoking," Tönle replied.

"I can see that. But why are they keeping you here? How old are you?"

"Over eighty."

"Where're you from?"

He didn't answer right away. He removed the pipe from his mouth and stared him in the face.

"It was near your town that I got wounded," said the guard, who had obviously been assigned this duty because he was unfit for service at the front. "Now it's all been destroyed."

"I know."

"I got wounded when we withdrew to set up a line of defense."

"Ah, *ja*," said Tönle, "does that mean it's been retaken by the Italians?"

Thus he learned that the Austrian offensive had been stopped and hurled back, that all the houses lay in ruins, and that the front now passed right behind his house and extended up through the meadows, pastures, woods, and mountains to the old border at the Passo dell'Agnella.

But no, maybe his house hadn't been destroyed, the house the old folks had built on a spot sheltered from storms and possibly from cannon fire.

A sad autumn came, without the colors that are so bright in our homeland; a gray drizzle fell on the world at war. Through the panes of the barred windows of the barracks, old Tönle Bintarn watched the rain and thought of the fireplace at home, the cherry tree on the roof, the other houses in the hamlet, the smoke from the chimneys, and what had been inside those houses: the living and the dead. And in that barracks filled with smells, futile voices, and dampness, time passed very slowly.

During that endless time, news arrived in the camp that the emperor Franz Josef was dead. Tönle remembered having once seen him at a military parade after maneuvers on the border with Russia; already he had looked old, with those long side-whiskers and thick, gray mustaches. He thought: And if he was already old when I was a soldier, who knows how old he is now. Maybe a hundred. So why had he fought this war? How could an old man of a hundred command soldiers, even if he's the emperor? It's not the emperors and kings who command. Then who does? The generals? The ministers? It seemed to him that maneuvers and military parades had been a game to entertain the emperor, and that the war, as he had seen on his mountains, was nothing but a game by other people more powerful than the emperor Franz Josef and King Victor Emmanuel.

Von Richer, the commandant in charge of the civilians interned in the camp, put a band of black silk on his left arm in sign of mourning, and for a week didn't speak even to the soldiers on duty; he gave his orders only with quick, curt gestures.

And the thin, gray, steady rain streaked the glass behind the iron bars from where old Tönle's eyes stared out, looking for any sign whatsoever of an impossible spring.

Ever so slowly Christmas was approaching; through the rare breaks in the gray, ragged clouds over the landscape and bare trees, Tönle was sometimes able to glimpse with yearning sadness the snow on the mountains west of Linz: he was thinking that behind those mountains there were still higher ones, that at a certain point the water of the rivers flowed down the other slope where there was sunshine, and there, in the mountains in the sunshine, was his house with the cherry tree on the roof.

At night, lying on a sack of shavings on his wooden bunk, he would stare with wide-open eyes into the darkness at the beams overhead, and always, toward dawn, he was assailed by a strong feeling of restlessness. He could hear the monotonous footsteps of the sentries, people talking in their sleep, the sighs, prayers, and curses of his barrack companions, and the crying of children in the women's section.

On one of these mornings, they sent him, along with others, to the station to unload cabbages from the freight cars for the camp kitchens. He went willingly because time went by more quickly when he had something to do. They worked for three hours, passing from hand to hand the big cabbages, which were packed into carts drawn by skinny nags covered with sores and discarded by the army. But when they were about at the end of the last carload of cabbages and the guards were relaxing by drinking beer in the station buffet, Tönle decided to leave, and without saying a word put on his jacket, pretended to urinate against a hedge, and then walked quickly through it and into the damp fields, which opened out before him.

He walked for a couple of hours trying to stay hidden by trees and ditches, then he proceeded calmly. On a road between fields he met an idiot boy driving a cart drawn by an old, broken-down horse; he spoke to him and got in the cart, and together they covered a good stretch of road; indeed, when he arrived at the farmhouse where the idiot lived with his mother, the woman invited him to stay if he wanted to and lend a hand with the work now that all the men were away in the war.

He stayed for a couple of days, but then continued on his way. He thought of following the river currents upstream to the watershed, then descending it. It wouldn't be the first time he had done it! Except that now his legs were so old, and there was the war, and he had to be careful not to get caught.

He walked, avoiding cities and the larger villages; he

stopped to do odd jobs in isolated houses halfway up the mountainside, and no one suspected him: he was only an old tramp of few words, trying somehow to live out his years.

Traveling like this, in two weeks he had covered some hundred kilometers and arrived in Trofaiach, near Leoben, and it was here, in a tavern, that an overzealous passing gendarme, seeing how shabby he looked and thinking he needed help, asked him for his identification papers. From his dilapidated wallet, Tönle took out the paper attesting his military service for the emperor Franz Josef, but this same paper, alas, also gave his place of birth, and now this was no longer in Austria. This aroused the suspicions of the gendarme, who wanted to know more, and it made him rummage among the other papers in the wallet: there was an employment certificate; the souvenir, with her photograph, of the requiem mass for his wife on the thirtieth day after her death; another photograph, typically American, of his emigrant sons; and also, unfortunately, the receipt for the sheep and dog that had been requisitioned from him.

The gendarme asked him to get up from the table, where he had sat down to drink a small beer, and took him to the police station in Leoben. There they interrogated him patiently and at length in a heated office while snow was falling outside.

But the stubborn old man refused to answer, or answered in his own way. They locked him up while awaiting verification, and when three or four days later the answer arrived, they put him on a train and sent him back to Katzenau, where Baron von Richer welcomed him with a scolding that deep down concealed both understanding and admiration.

Two days before Christmas, the gray drizzle falling on the camp changed to heavy wet snow, first mixing with the mud, then covering everything. The morning of 25 December, when Tönle, after wiping the misty panes with his hand, looked through the barred window, he read on the snow in front of the barracks, in large Gothic letters: FROHE WEIH-NACHTEN!

It had been done by a guard during the final watch of the night, while in the distance one heard the first village bells.

But while all this was going on, many other things were happening to Tönle's family and to our refugees in and beyond the Veneto plain.

By order of the prefect, the municipal center had been temporarily established in Noventa, and there mayor, councillors, town courier, and foresters were busily trying to track down or get news of our dispersed countrymen so as to register them, find them a place to live, and give them whatever assistance they needed, with the help of the civil and military authorities and committees set up for the purpose.

But it's also a fact that those of our people who had lost everything with the war did not always receive material aid, love, and understanding from their compatriots in the kingdom. Because of our old tradition of self-government, and because of their character, their strange antiquated tongue, their look of poverty, and their rustic and reserved way of doing things, our mountaineers were considered pro-Austrian, uncouth, and even accused of being traitors for having allowed the hated enemy to invade the sacred soil of the fatherland; as though women, old men, children, and the sick should have bared their chests to cannons and machine guns! And so the suspicion came naturally to them that some general had deliberately circulated rumors of "treason" on the part of our people, in order to conceal his own ineptitude and carelessness, and thus keep the blame from falling on his command and on his poorly led troops for the Austrian successes—which anyway were immediately contained when Cadorno ordered changes or replacements.

In short, when a couple of months after that May of 1916 it was possible to take a survey of the refugees, our old Tönle Bintarn was seen to be among the missing. He could not be located in any cottage in the Pedemontana, nor anywhere in the countryside toward the lagoons where our flocks had been wintering since time immemorial. Only Bepi Pûne, the boy who had had custody of Parlío's sheep and had been called up in the Sette Comuni battalion, reported having seen him climbing up toward the woods that day when everyone else was fleeing in the opposite direction.

From Noventa the mayor wrote to the Red Cross to ask if it were possible, through the Swiss Confederation, to have news from the enemy side. In Milan, the lawyer Bischofar's son, who had taken his family there and was living in poverty on the outskirts at Porta Ticinese, went to the Committee to Assist War Refugees, which was under the patronage of the Women's Lyceum, not to ask help for himself, but with personal data about our old man, sent by a friend in the hope that he would take an interest in the case. And so even the ladies of Milan got busy and through courts, the Red Cross, and various committees, it finally emerged that he was alive, in an Austrian detention camp not far from Linz; and it was possible to send news of him to his daughters and grandchildren housed in a camp in Varese, to his two sons in the Alpine troops now fighting near the Ortigara, and to the other three in America.

About a year later, on behalf of the Italian Red Cross and

the Women's Lyceum division in Milan, a priest from the canton of Ticino was allowed to visit the Katzenau camp to check on the condition of the interned civilians and propose to the Austrian authorities that women, children, and the sick be released and sent back to Italy, via Switzerland, in exchange for an equal number of wounded Austro-Hungarian prisoners, who should not, however, once recovered, be allowed to take up arms again.

Already in the month of July there had been an exchange and some hundred civilians had been able to return.

Baron von Richer, who was in charge of the internees and wore mourning for the death of Franz Josef, listened aloofly to the priest's proposal, although in his heart he was glad, since serious problems had arisen both for the food supply and the sanitary conditions in the camp.

The Swiss priest was allowed to walk around the camp and when during his inspection he saw our scornful old man sitting solitary and to one side, staring engrossed at some mullein leaves that he had spread out to dry in the sun so as to smoke them later in his black, encrusted, and saliva-stained pipe, he went closer to get a better look at him. He went still closer and the old man didn't look up, but seeing someone's shadow on the leaves, said, "Move, they have to dry."

Then the priest spoke up, asking him politely where he came from, how old he was, what he did, and how was his health. He made him repeat his name, wrote it down in his notebook, and left without getting any response when he said good-bye.

Hard to say why von Richer balked so much at the request that Tönle's name be included on the list for repatriation;

perhaps he had been singled out by the police, perhaps because they were afraid he might report something he had seen behind the front lines, perhaps because he had once been a soldier in the Imperial and Royal Army (and I think this was the main reason), or because he spoke Austrian and German dialects, as well as Czech, Hungarian, Croatian, Italian, and that peculiar language known as Cimbrian.

But the Swiss priest was at least as stubborn as Baron von Richer, and finally persuaded him to send for this strange, surly old man and hear what he had to say. In short, tight-lipped as he was, they managed to get him to speak, and in perfect German he said yes, he would go home, but there they must see to it that he got back his sheep and dog, which the soldiers had taken away from him, or rather that the gendarmes had sequestered after he'd been caught by the soldiers. He had a receipt. And as he said this, he took his wallet out of a well-hidden pocket in his fustian hunting jacket, and from it a folded piece of paper, which he spread out before them both, inviting them to read it.

Von Richer and the priest read it and looked at each other, then said yes. They would see to it that he got back his sheep and dog. But Tönle realized that this was a pitiful lie, even toward himself, and a smile, half ironical, half melancholy, a shepherd's smile, flickered in his eyes. Certainly the two of them didn't understand him, but his name was put on the repatriation list.

Copies of this list began traveling from one office to another, from Vienna to Rome, Geneva to Milan, recorded on protocols, stamped, and endorsed; and the covering letters verified, registered, and receipt acknowledged. Again the lists from the other side, checked off and compared.

Meanwhile, weeks and months went by, and the autumn of 1917 loomed. Tönle learned of an Italian offensive in our mountains, which failed: this was the battle of Mount Ortigara and became famous.

Again it started raining and time dragged on, as slow as muddy water. The Katzenau internees grew more and more emaciated and sad and short-tempered; the eyes of the children who called him grandpa became larger and larger, and the older ones always less playful. And now there were more frequent deaths, and they weren't like that of Franz Josef, almost a hundred years old, in his bed and big house. The news of Caporetto came and spread immediately, and it looked as though the war was about to end, but then came the news of the Piave and the war went on.

It was December and for days it had done nothing but rain; dampness and mildew were in the air throughout the Katzenau internment camp, in the barracks, in the sawdust bread, and in people's hearts. One day, by banging with an iron rod on a piece of railroad track hung on a scaffolding, they mustered the inmates.

They read out the names written on a list with many rubber stamps; those chosen were lined up to one side, told to collect what few miserable belongings they may have managed to keep, and at a tired pace and still under that monotonous drizzle, they were marched to the station, where an empty troop train stood waiting for them.

Meanwhile, the Milanese committee of the Red Cross had notified any traceable relatives that the train with the civilian internees would arrive at the Central Station at such and such a time on such and such a day, and they should be there to welcome them.

But the train was slow and the journey long, through

Salzburg and Innsbruck, Landeck and Feldkirch, where it finally entered Switzerland, and through Graubünden and Ticino, to arrive down in Milan a day later than expected.

It was night; the relatives who had been waiting all day, tired and chilled, had sought refuge in the waiting rooms, but most of them were in the rest areas prepared for soldiers in transit where, under the supervision of the Red Cross ladies, it was even possible to get a hot drink, a canvas cot, and a blanket with fleas and lice.

Amid rain, puffs of steam, whistles, and the screech of brakes, the troop train stopped on a remote siding. The Red Cross had been notified of the train's arrival only a few minutes before, and except for some railway workmen, there was no one waiting on the platform.

Numb and with stiff limbs from the long journey, with their wretched bundles and weak with hunger, the repatriated passengers helped each other to alight in small groups, while searching all around with their eyes for a friendly face that wasn't there.

SIX

Tönle Bintarn was among the first to get off, holding in his arms the little girl, whom he then turned over to her mother, and having no belongings with him and seeing nothing now to detain him, he set out at a determined pace, his extinguished pipe between his teeth, toward a dim light that he saw at the very end of the tracks and which might be the tail light of another train.

Instead it was a canteen for soldiers in transit. Inside it was warm and smoky, and pushing his way forward without bothering to be polite, he went up to the bar. A sergeant bluntly asked him what he was doing in here and where he came from. Still more bluntly, without mincing words, he told him where he came from and what he was looking for: tobacco for his pipe.

Meanwhile, a soldier approached from a group of others, staring at him. "Yes," he said, "it's him. Aren't you the shepherd we ordered to get out of the woods with his sheep three years ago when we were holding target practice up there in the mountains?" Tönle, too, stared at his face, and recognized the young artilleryman who had asked him about his sheep and the pastures because he himself was a shepherd in Sardinia. He felt as though he had recovered what he had lost. Now here's someone, he thought after a moment, that you can ask for a little tobacco, and talk to and be understood.

"Come on," said the soldier. "I'll buy you a drink."

But the sergeant butted in, saying that civilians weren't allowed in this place, which made the soldiers snicker in chorus and toss a few epithets in his direction that shut him up for good.

The two shepherds, reunited by an odd circumstance, went up to the bar, where the younger one ordered half a liter of wine and offered the old man a packet of five Tuscan cigars. He had been dreaming for a year now of tobacco like this, and crumbled half a cigar in the palm of his hand: he crammed a good portion into his pipe and put the rest in his mouth to chew.

The old man smoked slowly and with eager pleasure, he smoked and in a few words related his adventure and that of the sheep. Then the soldier also told what had been happening to him; whereupon the old man unstitched the hem of his jacket with his fingernails, took out a five-lira silver coin, and ordered more wine.

He felt his heart warmed after all that had happened, and having enjoyed his pipe and tobacco, he realized how hungry he was, and so he ordered bread and cheese and another liter of wine for the soldiers who had gathered around to listen.

Then the door of the canteen opened, and with a puff of fog and the smell of coal came a woman's voice, saying in sharp tones: "Is there an old man here, a civilian?"

"No-o," replied several voices. "No old men here."

What had happened was that when the Red Cross officials checked off the names on the list, the old man had not responded. They had immediately searched the whole station, and one of his daughters, who had come all the way from Varese, where she was a refugee, was disconsolate and burst into tears. "It's night, and he may have gone through the gates," the officials told her. "He will have gone into the city. Don't cry. You'll see, we'll find him tomorrow."

Morning came and the Sardinian soldier had to board a troop train to rejoin his regiment, near the Altipiano front. "Does your train go through Vicenza or Padua?" the old man asked him.

"I think so," he replied.

"Then I'll get on that train too."

And so, mingling with the soldiers, he boarded a livestock car; a patrol made the rounds and found everything in order, the engine whistled, the conductor signalled all clear with his lantern, and the train departed with a clanging of buffers and the raucous singing of the soldiers.

The train chugged along all day across the plain, passing cities and rivers, stopping sometimes in the open countryside, sometimes outside the stations. At Vicenza it passed slowly between divisions of soldiers lined up on benches and other trains loaded with war supplies; the old man peered through the little window high up in the car toward the mountains, which looked white amid the clouds, and thought: Soon I'll be home.

The troop train stopped at Cittadella, and here the boisterous soldiers got off, after making him a gift of tobacco, cigars, hard biscuits, a few cans of meat, and a worn-out haversack. Without letting himself be seen by the duty patrol, and having said good-bye to the Sardinian shepherd, who called him Uncle Antonio and addressed him with the formal *voi*, he slipped between the hedges and the wooden fence and emerged in the open countryside.

He knew that the shepherds' road passed not far from this walled city, the road that for centuries had joined mountains and Venetian lagoons, and so he cut across the fields westward until he came upon it near the banks of the Brenta. But night soon fell, suddenly, and he stopped in a hut of cornstalks, stretched out on the straw, lit his pipe, and after he had smoked, fell asleep, tired and almost happy because of his regained independence and freedom, his home, and all the other things that he now felt were close at hand.

He was aroused in the middle of the night by strange voices; instantly he was wide awake and cocked an ear, without moving. He couldn't make out what the people outside were saying in low voices: it didn't sound like an Italian dialect or even a German one. He kept still and only opened his eyes when two soldiers came in the hut and lit a match. They laughed at seeing this old man crouching there, his eyes as alert as a nocturnal animal's; one put his hand in a pocket of his jacket, took out a package of cigarettes, and threw it to him. The old man didn't know in what language to thank them; they went out, spoke with the ones who were waiting outside, and disappeared in the night.

None of this could have surprised the old man, except he had no way of knowing that this was a British patrol from the Royal Garrison Artillery, which had arrived in the area after the disaster at Caporetto.

Before dawn he sat up, put a piece of hard biscuit in his mouth to moisten it with saliva before chewing it, lit his pipe, and went out, to arrive at the bank of the Brenta, which he planned to follow upstream toward the gray, cloud-covered mountains rising to the north. And thus it was that in the first light of dawn he once again heard the sound of cannons.

Meanwhile, it having been confirmed that he had got on the train at Katzenau, made the transit through Switzerland, been present when the list was checked at Chiasso, and had arrived in Milan, as the little girl's mother testified, it was obvious that the place he must have vanished from was the Central Station. This was what the Red Cross authorities notified our mayor in Noventa, the various committees, the mayors of the municipalities in the Pedemontana, the carabinieri, the police, the roadblocks. The last to be notified were his two sons Matío and Petar, who had luckily survived the battles to take the Ortigara and the ones to hold Mount Fior. Now, with their battalion, they had fallen back to the "last-ditch" defense line along the cliffs overhanging the Brenta Canal. Colonel Magliano sent for the older of the two—the command was in a cave under the Sasso Rosso—and issuing him a special three-day pass (truly special since, given the situation, all leaves and passes had been revoked, but Colonel Magliano had a good memory and he recalled that peculiar old man), told Petar to go and look for his father, who had almost certainly arrived in the area.

As Tönle approached the mountains, hearing ever more distinctly, as the day wore on, the sounds of cannons, he walked slowly, seemingly absentminded but actually highly attentive to what was going on around him. He avoided carabinieri, patrols, and officers, but didn't mind trudging along beside divisions that were marching in ranks up secondary roads toward the woods. Long lines of trucks and armored vehicles were ascending by the main roads.

Having avoided Bassano and Marostica, while skirting Vallonara and Crosara, he was now headed for Santa Caterina, and when he passed the stone that marked the boundary between the Venetian Republic and the Sette Comuni, he gave a sigh of relief: it was almost over and tomorrow he'd be home.

Climbing toward Conco along a mule track among chestnut and walnut trees, he followed an infantry regiment on its way to the Altipiano. Almost all of them were Sardinian soldiers, who told him during the prescribed rest period that they had been in these woods and mountains for over a year; they had fought on Mount Fior and Mount Zebio. He got them to explain where the trenches ran, and how the town and hamlets were doing—in short, whether they were occupied by Germans or Italians.

Then he understood clearly that in June of the previous year, a few days after the Austrians had taken him away with the sheep, Italian soldiers had reoccupied his hamlet and the imperial troops had withdrawn to the Porchecche.

While they were thus conversing quietly, they were approached by a tall, lean captain, with a lively look in his eye. "Uncle," this captain said suddenly, and at his voice the soldiers started to get to their feet, but he stopped them with a wave of his hand. "Uncle, where do you want to go?"

"Home," said Tönle, taking his pipe from his mouth. "To my house."

"Where do you live?"

Tönle Bintarn told him the name of the hamlet, and Captain Emilio Lussu smiled sadly. "The Austrians retook it a few days ago. Go back to the plain," he added, "and wait until it's all over. Don't you have any family?"

"Battalion, shoulder knapsacks! Forward march!" was

heard at the head of the column that had been resting. And then, "Captain Lussu, round up the stragglers!"

Grumbling and wisecracking, the soldiers hoisted their packs on their backs and set off again toward the sound of the cannons; Tönle did not follow them. But neither did he turn back; he let them go ahead and saw the tall, upright captain wave good-bye to him, a wave that meant: Go back.

It was beginning to get dark and the air was turning cold and damp; he started walking again, following a path along the hillside that led to a small stable where animals were sheltered in the summer; there was a pile of dry leaves in one corner, soft and rustling beech leaves; he lay down and covered himself with them for protection from the cold. He was thinking that at a certain hour of the night he would set out again toward home: even going slowly and cautiously to avoid the soldiers, he'd be there in three hours.

He rewound his watch, ate some of what was left in the haversack, lit his pipe, and waited for the time to pass. When carefully he lit a match to look at his watch, it was three o'clock. Shortly thereafter, he rose, brushed off the leaves, and went out.

The clouds had all drifted down toward the plain, and the sky over the mountains looked cold and clear, and the cold and the many stars acutely reminded him of the winter sky over the roof of his house, with the smell of wood smoke, and the snow, and the Christmas songs. He thought: It really must be Christmas by now.

Propped against the stone wall was a stick that some cowherd had left behind in the grazing season; he took it and kept going. He walked at a fast pace, the pace with which he had crossed the borders many years ago. He avoided hamlets, military encampments, mobilized work crews, large-caliber gun emplacements, roadblocks. But to do this took more time than he had foreseen, and when he arrived at the edge of the great dark woods that shut our mountains off from the plain, it was already daylight.

In the woods, he could now walk more safely, and he took the high path along the boundary line between two communes, leading to Mount Sprunch. But he found it impossible to pass beyond a certain point: he went round and round and always ran into either a battery hidden among fir trees, or a rearguard trench, or a tangle of barbed wire. Whereupon he abandoned all caution and entered the Barental. He was stopped by a second lieutenant in the mountain artillery, taken to battery headquarters, searched, and interrogated.

The captain was unable to make him see reason; nor could the old man persuade the captain.

"Listen," the captain finally said to the lieutenant, "we're wasting time here and at any moment we may get the order to open fire; just listen to all those guns toward the Valbella. Take this pigheaded old man to the lookout, let him see his house through the periscope, and then to hell with him!"

The two of them went to the Nisce observation post; the lieutenant had him explain the location of his house, and then aiming the periscope, invited him to look through the eyepieces.

Tönle immediately saw that there was no cherry tree on the roof, and not even a roof, and the walls cracked and blackened, and the kitchen garden in front uprooted, with deep holes that instead of rich black soil had brought to the surface stones white as bones. That's not my house, he thought. But then as he went on gazing in silence, seeing the Moor behind and the ruins of the other houses in the hamlet, and the terraced fields, and Grabo and what was left of Prunnele in front, he realized that it had all once been there. From behind Grabo he saw four puffs of smoke suddenly arise and then many Austrian soldiers crouching low as they ran.

But the lieutenant, who was watching with binoculars, also saw the four puffs of smoke and the soldiers, and pushed the old man away with his arm; he reached for the telephone, called the battery command, and told them about the shots. Four big guns close by immediately opened rapid fire, and the shells fell and exploded around the house and on the meadow behind it.

It was 24 December 1917, and the Austrians had begun a breakthrough drive to outflank Mount Grappa and the Piave. All the cannons on both sides started firing, and the Austrian and Hungarian forces went on the offensive in an effort to reach Venice, as the emperor Karl, who was watching the operation with satisfaction from the Melette heights, had promised them. The Italian regiments counterattacked to retake trenches and redoubts; men were cut down by machine guns, and yellow clouds of poison gas settled in the hollows, devastated by barbed wire and dried-up trees. The snow turned gray with smoke and red with blood.

Now no one paid any attention to Tönle Bintarn, the soldiers had other things to do; sitting in a corner of the observation post and with his spent pipe between his teeth, he heard the shells exploding around him and passing over his head. When he thought to look through a slit, he saw the town below beyond the meadows. But there were no more meadows: snow, stones, barbed wire, and the corpses of soldiers were all mixed together. Where the town should have been there was a pile of rocks; nor were there any tall trees left over the graves in the cemetery behind the church.

The soldiers were still intent on what they were doing, and so he went slowly away by the communication trench, and when he reached the depths of the woods he left the trench and slowly went down the mountains, as the other refugees had done in May of the previous year. This time, too, there was the roar of cannon fire, flames, soldiers going up, ambulances and stretcher bearers going down. But by now there was nothing left down there to destroy, and nothing by which to live.

Tönle walked slowly through the Camporossignolo woods, at a tired pace, meeting the soldiers going up silently toward the battle, and hearing the cries of the wounded on stretchers. His old fustian hunting jacket still smelled of salt and sheep.

He left the woods, road, and path, and stopped to spend another night in a sheepfold hidden amid cytisus and alders, in a gorge where weasels found shelter, and cats that had reverted to the wild.

The noise of the battle had somewhat abated, but at dawn he was aroused from his torpid slumber by a ceaseless uproar that grew louder and louder; he realized that all the cannons, including the large-caliber ones positioned on the lower edges of the Altipiano, were firing nonstop. He recalled the image of what he had seen through the instrument at the Nisce observation post and crept into a corner of the straw like a lamb chilled to the bone, not out of fear certainly, but pity.

During the day, like sudden gusts of wind, the battle

intensified and diminished, and it was only toward evening that it subsided a little.

Then Tönle Bintarn emerged from his shelter and set out for the plain. He had decided to look for some village that was still inhabited, ask about the refugees from our area, find his daughters and grandchildren, and wait for the end. At a stream he drank thirstily and bathed his face. He climbed down steep paths, sometimes having to hold onto the branches of trees or the roots of bushes; he crossed meadows glittering with hoarfrost, and cultivated plots hardened by the cold. Then the air suddenly turned milder, like spring.

Unwittingly he had come to that strange spot at the foot of our mountains and before the beginning of the great plain, where sweet figs and muscat grapes ripen and olive trees grow.

He felt well now, there were no more sounds of battle, but only a light breeze through the branches of the olive trees. Evening came on and even the plain toward the sea turned brighter: the sky took on the color of the sea. He sat down under an olive tree, wound his watch without realizing that the hours that had gone by that day were those of Christmas; he lit his pipe, leaned back against the tree, saying aloud, "It feels like a spring evening," and remembered the one many years ago when at the edge of the woods he had waited for the shadows of night to make the cherry tree fade on the roof before going home.

The next morning the fighting was over, as when a storm runs out of clouds and thunderbolts. The exhausted soldiers rested at their devastated positions and the wounded were transported behind the lines. Lieutenant Filippo Sacchi had to report to Colonel Scandolara at the headquarters of the Ninth Alpine Group, to deliver and pick up dispatches for the Fifty-second Division; since it was a calm and beautiful day, he had the idea of stopping on his way to visit the abbey of Campese and pay his respects to the tomb of the poet Teofilo Folengo.

He was going along, lost in thought, when, in the vicinity of San Michele, where Benedictine monks centuries ago had planted those olive trees, he saw an old man sitting calmly propped against a tree, with a pipe in his hand. "Good morning!" he said. But there was no answer. Maybe he's deaf, he thought, and waved to him. Still there was no response, and when he got close he realized he was dead. He looked around, and at first saw no one; then he heard footsteps on the road above and called out. A rather ragged soldier appeared, a helmet on his head and a cape over his shoulder. "Come down," the lieutenant told him, "we've got to do something. There's an old man dead."

I had been in the woods gathering firewood for the winter and there was no one at home to answer the telephone. I didn't know.

As on other evenings, before supper, I went to see Gigi. As I walked, I thought of his illness, which day by day was diminishing his strength but not his will to live. It's extraordinary, I thought.

In the fields around the hamlet they were hoeing potatoes and the chimneys were smoking from fire for the polenta. I was also thinking of the story I had finished and a few other ones I meant to tell him.

Greeting people along the way, I reached his house: it was all closed up, there were no chairs outside on the porch, and his car was not under the birch trees.

With a heavy heart and a lump in my throat, I went to the Nappas for confirmation. "He had to leave in a hurry because he felt ill," they told me. "They tried to phone your house but you weren't in."

The first shadows were falling across the mountains, and I sat before the door and looked at the cow on the Moor, as though he were still there with me.

Asiago, in the long winter of 1977–78